UNDONE

(A Cora Shields Mystery —Book One)

BLAKE PIERCE

Blake Pierce

Blake Pierce is the USA Today bestselling author of the RILEY PAGE mystery series, which includes seventeen books. Blake Pierce is also the author of the MACKENZIE WHITE mystery series, comprising fourteen books; of the AVERY BLACK mystery series, comprising six books; of the KERI LOCKE mystery series, comprising five books; of the MAKING OF RILEY PAIGE mystery series, comprising six books; of the KATE WISE mystery series, comprising seven books; of the CHLOE FINE psychological suspense mystery, comprising six books; of the JESSIE HUNT psychological suspense thriller series, comprising twenty six books; of the AU PAIR psychological suspense thriller series, comprising three books; of the ZOE PRIME mystery series, comprising six books; of the ADELE SHARP mystery series, comprising sixteen books, of the EUROPEAN VOYAGE cozy mystery series, comprising six books; of the new LAURA FROST FBI suspense thriller, comprising eleven books (and counting); of the new ELLA DARK FBI suspense thriller, comprising fourteen books (and counting); of the A YEAR IN EUROPE cozy mystery series, comprising nine books, of the AVA GOLD mystery series, comprising six books (and counting); of the RACHEL GIFT mystery series, comprising ten books (and counting); of the VALERIE LAW mystery series, comprising nine books (and counting); of the PAIGE KING mystery series, comprising eight books (and counting); of the MAY MOORE mystery series, comprising eleven books (and counting); the CORA SHIELDS mystery series, comprising five books (and counting); and of the NICKY LYONS mystery series, comprising five books (and counting).

An avid reader and lifelong fan of the mystery and thriller genres, Blake loves to hear from you, so please email at blake {AT} blakepierceauthor.com to stay in touch.

BOOKS BY BLAKE PIERCE

NICKY LYONS MYSTERY SERIES
ALL MINE (Book #1)
ALL HIS (Book #2)
ALL HE SEES (Book #3)
ALL ALONE (Book #4)
ALL FOR ONE (Book #5)

CORA SHIELDS MYSTERY SERIES
UNDONE (Book #1)
UNWANTED (Book #2)
UNHINGED (Book #3)
UNSAID (Book #4)
UNGLUED (Book #5)

MAY MOORE SUSPENSE THRILLER
NEVER RUN (Book #1)
NEVER TELL (Book #2)
NEVER LIVE (Book #3)
NEVER HIDE (Book #4)
NEVER FORGIVE (Book #5)
NEVER AGAIN (Book #6)
NEVER LOOK BACK (Book #7)
NEVER FORGET (Book #8)
NEVER LET GO (Book #9)
NEVER PRETEND (Book #10)
NEVER HESITATE (Book #11)

PAIGE KING MYSTERY SERIES
THE GIRL HE PINED (Book #1)
THE GIRL HE CHOSE (Book #2)
THE GIRL HE TOOK (Book #3)
THE GIRL HE WISHED (Book #4)
THE GIRL HE CROWNED (Book #5)
THE GIRL HE WATCHED (Book #6)
THE GIRL HE WANTED (Book #7)
THE GIRL HE CLAIMED (Book #8)

GIRL, HUNTED (Book #3)
GIRL, SILENCED (Book #4)
GIRL, VANISHED (Book 5)
GIRL ERASED (Book #6)
GIRL, FORSAKEN (Book #7)
GIRL, TRAPPED (Book #8)
GIRL, EXPENDABLE (Book #9)
GIRL, ESCAPED (Book #10)
GIRL, HIS (Book #11)
GIRL, LURED (Book #12)
GIRL, MISSING (Book #13)
GIRL, UNKNOWN (Book #14)

LAURA FROST FBI SUSPENSE THRILLER
ALREADY GONE (Book #1)
ALREADY SEEN (Book #2)
ALREADY TRAPPED (Book #3)
ALREADY MISSING (Book #4)
ALREADY DEAD (Book #5)
ALREADY TAKEN (Book #6)
ALREADY CHOSEN (Book #7)
ALREADY LOST (Book #8)
ALREADY HIS (Book #9)
ALREADY LURED (Book #10)
ALREADY COLD (Book #11)

EUROPEAN VOYAGE COZY MYSTERY SERIES
MURDER (AND BAKLAVA) (Book #1)
DEATH (AND APPLE STRUDEL) (Book #2)
CRIME (AND LAGER) (Book #3)
MISFORTUNE (AND GOUDA) (Book #4)
CALAMITY (AND A DANISH) (Book #5)
MAYHEM (AND HERRING) (Book #6)

ADELE SHARP MYSTERY SERIES
LEFT TO DIE (Book #1)
LEFT TO RUN (Book #2)
LEFT TO HIDE (Book #3)
LEFT TO KILL (Book #4)
LEFT TO MURDER (Book #5)
LEFT TO ENVY (Book #6)

LEFT TO LAPSE (Book #7)
LEFT TO VANISH (Book #8)
LEFT TO HUNT (Book #9)
LEFT TO FEAR (Book #10)
LEFT TO PREY (Book #11)
LEFT TO LURE (Book #12)
LEFT TO CRAVE (Book #13)
LEFT TO LOATHE (Book #14)
LEFT TO HARM (Book #15)
LEFT TO RUIN (Book #16)

THE AU PAIR SERIES
ALMOST GONE (Book#1)
ALMOST LOST (Book #2)
ALMOST DEAD (Book #3)

ZOE PRIME MYSTERY SERIES
FACE OF DEATH (Book#1)
FACE OF MURDER (Book #2)
FACE OF FEAR (Book #3)
FACE OF MADNESS (Book #4)
FACE OF FURY (Book #5)
FACE OF DARKNESS (Book #6)

A JESSIE HUNT PSYCHOLOGICAL SUSPENSE SERIES
THE PERFECT WIFE (Book #1)
THE PERFECT BLOCK (Book #2)
THE PERFECT HOUSE (Book #3)
THE PERFECT SMILE (Book #4)
THE PERFECT LIE (Book #5)
THE PERFECT LOOK (Book #6)
THE PERFECT AFFAIR (Book #7)
THE PERFECT ALIBI (Book #8)
THE PERFECT NEIGHBOR (Book #9)
THE PERFECT DISGUISE (Book #10)
THE PERFECT SECRET (Book #11)
THE PERFECT FAÇADE (Book #12)
THE PERFECT IMPRESSION (Book #13)
THE PERFECT DECEIT (Book #14)
THE PERFECT MISTRESS (Book #15)
THE PERFECT IMAGE (Book #16)

ONCE HUNTED (Book #5)
ONCE PINED (Book #6)
ONCE FORSAKEN (Book #7)
ONCE COLD (Book #8)
ONCE STALKED (Book #9)
ONCE LOST (Book #10)
ONCE BURIED (Book #11)
ONCE BOUND (Book #12)
ONCE TRAPPED (Book #13)
ONCE DORMANT (Book #14)
ONCE SHUNNED (Book #15)
ONCE MISSED (Book #16)
ONCE CHOSEN (Book #17)

MACKENZIE WHITE MYSTERY SERIES
BEFORE HE KILLS (Book #1)
BEFORE HE SEES (Book #2)
BEFORE HE COVETS (Book #3)
BEFORE HE TAKES (Book #4)
BEFORE HE NEEDS (Book #5)
BEFORE HE FEELS (Book #6)
BEFORE HE SINS (Book #7)
BEFORE HE HUNTS (Book #8)
BEFORE HE PREYS (Book #9)
BEFORE HE LONGS (Book #10)
BEFORE HE LAPSES (Book #11)
BEFORE HE ENVIES (Book #12)
BEFORE HE STALKS (Book #13)
BEFORE HE HARMS (Book #14)

AVERY BLACK MYSTERY SERIES
CAUSE TO KILL (Book #1)
CAUSE TO RUN (Book #2)
CAUSE TO HIDE (Book #3)
CAUSE TO FEAR (Book #4)
CAUSE TO SAVE (Book #5)
CAUSE TO DREAD (Book #6)

KERI LOCKE MYSTERY SERIES
A TRACE OF DEATH (Book #1)
A TRACE OF MURDER (Book #2)

CHAPTER ONE

Cora nearly fell—her arm flinging out threatened to yank her shoulder from its socket. She hissed in pain as her fingers desperately gripped the concrete windowsill of the old, abandoned industrial building.

A static-filled voice over the receiver in her ear said, *"Only five minutes, Cora. Do you see him?"*

She didn't reply, conserving her energy and breathing heavily as fear prickled up her spine. Only five minutes—she'd taken too long, far too long. She shot a quick look down into the asphalt parking lot covered in overgrown weeds, grass poking through the tarmac cracks. No cars except for the one she and her partner had brought with them and the two large, black SUVs parked at the base of the building.

The SUVs belonged to routine security according to the corporation that owned the building.

But it wasn't the security she was interested in.

It was the man who paid their salaries.

They all *knew* what Desmond Rike got up to in his spare time. They all knew what he did to those girls he took with him, but they all turned a blind eye.

Technically, Cora and Agent Brady, her partner, weren't supposed to breech the building until the warrant showed up. The three-gun thugs at the entrance had made extra sure of that, along with the security cameras. But Cora knew they didn't have time—the sun reflecting off the windows was fading fast.

It was five minutes before sunset. Mr. Rike killed his victims *just* as the sun disappeared. An offering, they'd discovered, based on his little sun-worshiping cult.

For a moment, she dangled there, holding on with one arm, her left knee bouncing against the window below her. She exhaled shakily, feeling her nerves tingle. Small spurts of fear dabbed up her spine and whispered little threats in her subconscious, but she refocused. Her brow was slick, her arms were in pain, and she was twelve stories in the air, so she didn't look down a second time.

Cora had always hated heights.

But one of the benefits of her training—especially back in the

Navy, before joining the FBI—was that facing one's fears was a minimum requirement. There was at least an eighty percent dropout rate from BUDS and SEAL training.

And that was from the cream of the crop. The best of the best.

Cora had never considered herself the best at anything. She was simply stubborn.

Stubborn enough to refuse to let go of the windowsill. She pulled herself higher, her heart pounding wildly, her face coming in line with the next window now. She gripped the concrete ledge with both hands, arms still straining beneath her jacket sleeves. She let out a shuddering sigh, peering into the dark halls beyond the translucent glass.

A couple more men with guns were moving through the halls. She winced, ducked her head, and waited for them to pass. As she did, her ear receiver crackled again.

"Agent Shields!" a different voice this time, far angrier. *"Dammit, Agent Shields. Reply—now!"*

Cora winced. The deputy director didn't sound very happy. She moved towards the window she'd spotted from below. The only one on the east side of the building with a window left slightly ajar. She reached the window, pushing it open with the back of her hand.

"Agent Shields! We are ten minutes out. Hold position. Do you hear me? Hold position!" The voice over the radio only seemed to increase in volume the more she ignored it.

Granted, she had a lot of experience ignoring Deputy Director Malcolm Ogden. Director Ogden had never much liked Cora.

The feeling was certainly mutual.

The man didn't just play by the book. He worked by it, slept by it, took it to bed with him, wined and dined it, and everything in between.

Cora, on the other hand, had never been much of a reader.

She clicked off her radio receiver. The line went silent. Much better.

Now she could focus. Only a few minutes before another body would drop. Already, this psycho had taken out four young women.

She wasn't about to stand by for the sake of measly protocol while another was killed.

Her small, wiry frame allowed her to slip slowly through the open window, spilling onto the floor and falling into a crouch. She moved silently, on the balls of her feet, traversing down the quiet hall. Her ears were perked, listening for the sound of footsteps.

Cora's auburn hair was cut close, shaved completely on the left side and shoulder length on the right. Not exactly the hairdo of a girly girl, but Cora had never been accused of wearing pink or being in touch with her emotions. She wasn't unattractive—more than one of her old platoon mates had taken a shot. She'd taken passes of her own in return. But she certainly had never been described as *cute*. Her features were too sharp: her cheekbones high, her nose straight, her eyes cold gray, like the seas she'd patrolled for two tours in her mid- to late-twenties.

Her hand extended, braced against a wooden door as her other hand gripped her sidearm. The tattoos along her forearm twisted into her sleeve, standing out against taut but lean muscles.

In her twenties, Cora hadn't needed to work for a lean physique. Now, pushing thirty-one, she had a two-hour morning workout ritual she kept to religiously—not just because it kept back the poundage— but other, far darker demons were held at bay, at least somewhat, thanks to the endorphin rush.

The hinges creaked slowly as she pushed the door open. She gripped her weapon, swallowing. Her eyes moved about the empty and sparse room. An old office chair toppled. No desks. A few wires jutting out from empty sockets in the wall.

After a quick, cursory sweep, she moved to the next room. Again, empty.

Five more doors in the hall. He would be on one of the higher levels. That's what he always did. The last three victims he'd taken to a penthouse, to a clocktower, and to the top of an old cathedral.

Mr. Rike had made his money on Wall Street. But the man hadn't been satisfied with the bank account of a god. He'd wanted the worship of one as well. His little cult had been bought or bribed. He was charismatic and good-looking—they always were.

The best predators were the ones that were nice to look at. They could distract their prey with the superficial until it was too late.

She scowled, remembering the last body she'd found at the base of the cathedral, amidst the tombstones of the attached graveyard. He pushed them to their deaths. Rike had called it, in his secret meetings with his acolytes, *the plummet of Ra.*

Cora scowled, her sea-gray eyes storming as she moved to the next set of doors. And then, she heard movement.

She went still, moving quietly back against the wall. The door was suddenly opened. A couple of men in black suits pushed into the room, moving on to the next door. She stood quiet as the door swung past her, shielding her in shadow and creating a small alcove.

She caught faint strands of muttering.

"Think he's done her in yet?" one of them was saying, sounding uncomfortable with the concept.

The other grunted. "Meh. Didn't hear nothing yet from upstairs. Usually they scream."

"S-scream? Shit...I mean," he swallowed, then continued, "I...Okay."

The second, older guard snorted. "Don't think about it. Just do your job."

The first man replied, but his voice was muffled again as the two guards moved into the opposite room, continuing their lazy search pattern.

Cora waited until they had passed. And then she slipped out from behind the angled alcove the closing door had formed and hurried forward, hastening towards the set of stairs against the far wall.

Upstairs. The guard had said no noise from upstairs.

She was running out of time.

And so, she did. Start running, that is.

She broke into a sprint, while still attempting her best to move quietly, but this was growing futile. She heard the sound of voices behind her, no yelling yet. No bullets. Just alarm. They had heard her, no doubt, but by the sound of things they hadn't seen her yet. She reached the stairs, ducking around the corner, and taking them two at a time before anyone managed to call out after her.

There was no hesitation as she reached the next floor, racing forward, her feet flying across the cold concrete. This floor was labeled *14,* judging by the large, laminated sign on the right side of the stairwell. The red and white plastic was chipping, though, due to old age.

Cora wasn't hesitant any longer. She hastened rapidly forward, her feet flying over the bare concrete. The carpets had been ripped up. Ahead, she spotted a large glass door as if leading into a conference room. Two more men stood in front of the door.

She winced, but didn't slow, covering the distance between them—about thirty feet—rapidly.

The two men were shifting nervously, clearly uncomfortable as they listened to the sound of weeping in the room behind them. The sobs and the pleading were distraction enough.

She didn't pull her firearm, though. Already, she'd broken more than one rule in entering the building without an approved warrant. Technically, they hadn't *known* that Mr. Rike's victim was with him.

4

But it had been an educated guess. Cora and her partner had been tracking this killer long enough to know his patterns and habits. He'd always been careful, leaving the scene of the crime without a trace of evidence. It had been a clever deduction from Agent Brady, her partner, who had managed to tie a bank account of Rike's to the hotel next to the cathedral where one of the bodies had been discovered.

The sound of Cora's footfalls only registered by the time she'd covered half the distance. The men in suits looked up suddenly. Their eyes widened, eyebrows shot up, and hands darted for guns.

She didn't wait. Twenty feet. Ten. Guns in hand. Five feet. Aiming. A curse—

She slammed into them. A stiff and calloused hand directly to the throat of the man on the left. And a knee below the belt of the man on the right, swinging at full force. Both men went down with distinct but discernible sounds like leaking balloons.

She paused long enough to grab their weapons. Dissembling them both in a few quick motions, she tossed the clips off into a side room, ejected the live rounds, caught the bullets, and flung them in the other direction before dropping the deconstructed pieces of the weapons on the concrete. With a final kick, sending the pieces skittering past the groaning men, Cora lowered her shoulder.

As she did, she felt a sudden jolt of pain in her shoulder. Her thoughts tugged in her subconscious, attempting to lead her down a separate path...

She winced for a moment, her forearm braced against the streaked and smudged glass door. Her breath came in rapid pants and panic began to rise in her.

She was no longer standing in an industrial building in West Virginia.

No longer standing over the writhing forms of men in pain, but very much alive.

For a split-second, a brief instant, she was back in desert sand. Could smell the heat. Taste the salt of the ocean water on her lips. Could see the two dead figures on the ground, their blood pooling out beneath them like red glass. She could hear the sound of gunfire. Of her SEAL commander barking orders as she attempted to push through the pain of a gunshot wound in her arm.

One of the few female SEALs to ever make it through BUDS, Cora had lived a life proving twice as much to twice as many. At least, that's how it had felt.

5

She never complained though. That would have only increased the difficulty with her squad.

Now, standing there, the memory came back in a sudden burst. The pain, the blood, the first two kills—she'd shot them both without them ever having seen her, rising from the surf like a ghost at night.

And then...

Just as quickly, she was back.

She exhaled shakily, closing her eyes, and opening them, breathing deeply. She shook her head, sending droplets of sweat flicking from the unshaved portion of her hair.

The pain in her shoulder, her arm, memories of wounds, faded.

To an outsider, anyone watching, it might have seemed like the briefest of hesitations. A second or two to gather her breath.

But for Cora, it was as if someone set fire to her mind, watched it burn, then rebuilt it again, only to threaten the blaze at some other time, again and again and again.

She grit her teeth, wincing in frustration as she shoved through the doorway and emerged in the room she'd taken for a conference hall.

She'd been right.

Lacquered wooden tables shaped like a horseshoe lined the walls. And there, at the far end of the room, an open window.

She felt the sudden breeze and felt the way the air caressed her warm skin, brushing through the room. But her eyes were now fixed on the two figures by the window. It was a large, sliding window, nearly floor to ceiling. The metal blinds were shifting and rattling from the wind, but also from the struggling figures.

Both of them wore white robes. One of them had—of all strange things—a golden crown perched on his head. A handsome man, with dark, curly hair and green eyes. His olive skin suggested much time spent in the sun or in tanning salons.

Now, he was speaking in a soothing, cajoling voice that didn't at all match with his straining muscles, his violence as he tried to shove the woman out the window. "It is the will of the great star!" he said, in that attempt at a calming voice. "The will of its guide—please, Zaina! Do what I ask. Trust me!"

The young woman, though, was no longer as enamored as she'd once likely been with her cult leader. Young and in her mid-twenties, the woman was bucking and thrashing, trying to rip her arms out of the cold, steely grip of Desmond Rike.

The billionaire killer was laughing now, shaking his head side to

6

side, his perfect blonde hair swishing in the open window. "Come now," he murmured. "What's the point of resist—"

He caught himself, turning sharply.

Cora realized he must have spotted her reflection in the glass. She was already moving. Again, she left her gun in its holster. There was no clean shot while the two of them grappled by an open window. But she hastened forward now, sprinting towards the back of Rike as he turned.

The moment his perfect, green eyes settled on her, his plucked eyebrows shot up towards that silly little, golden-leafed crown of his.

He tried to protest, to say *something,* but it was futile. She slammed into him with a shout, her shoulder driving into his stomach. At the same time, though, she couldn't focus on subduing him. First things first: prioritize the scene.

She reached *past* him, snatching at his would-be victim. The young woman screamed as a new hand latched on her wrist. But Cora pulled, sharply, yanking her past the window and into the safety of the rigid, concrete wall.

Rike was cursing, though, reaching for a weapon of his own.

Now, though, Cora had a clear line of sight.

Her own gun sprang into her hand. Her other hand still gripped the woman, while Rike's other hand held her opposite arm in a deadly game of tug-of-war.

His eyes widened in panic as he froze suddenly, hand inside his waistband, going for his weapon. Cora spotted the glint of metal.

Rike swallowed, blinked. "Y-you can't be up here," he murmured.

Cora glared back. "Hands up. *Now.* Stop touching her."

She felt another flash of memory. Another distant horizon dawning once again in her mind. But she suppressed the thought and gave her full attention to the moment at hand.

She didn't feel fear or anxiety. Not now. Not in this moment.

Bad guys weren't the problem. Bad guys rarely scared her. No, not even after that brief stint in a prison in Cyprus. She'd been tortured and survived, been beaten and survived, been harmed in unimaginable ways and while her body still carried the scars, her psyche had lost most of its fear.

The thing that really *did* scare her, though...

The victims.

Not being able to save them.

Arriving too late.

In the SEALs, her job had been to kill bad guys and protect the soldiers on her right and left. In the FBI, it was to stop the bad guys while saving their would-be victims. A slightly different responsibility set.

She found it fulfilling, but more frightening.

And now, she had her hand firmly on the victim's shoulder. Her other hand didn't shake as she pointed the weapon at the billionaire serial killer's forehead.

He swallowed, still fumbling for the gun in his waistband. The barrel flashed. He slipped his finger into the trigger guard.

Her eyes narrowed. "Don't," she said simply. "You're not fast enough. Hands up, Rike."

At the use of his name, his eyes widened even further. He shot a look out the window. In the distance now, Cora thought she could hear the sound of approaching sirens.

Rike bit his lip. He didn't look nearly so handsome or charming anymore.

"P-please," he said, slowly. "She was trespassing. I found her here. She was trying to attack me!"

"Shut up, hands up."

The woman was crying now.

Rike let out a faint, world-weary sigh. Then his eyes narrowed superciliously beneath his golden crown. His lip curled into a sneer, and he suddenly pulled his gun.

It didn't even make it past the waistband.

Before he could even blink...

Two shots.

She was already turning as Desmond Rike's corpse toppled to the ground.

She gripped the woman's arm. She whispered, "It's going to be okay. You're safe now, ma'am. I promise you. You're safe."

As the sirens approached, though, Cora wondered if the same could be said for her.

She winced, finally shooting a glance towards Rike's corpse. She sighed. Entering without a warrant, against the direct command of a superior, no *actual* probable cause, only hunches and guesses...

She sighed.

Saved a life, but still in trouble.

Par for the course, she supposed.

CHAPTER TWO

Cora sat uncomfortably in front of her supervisor's desk, her foot tapping against the floor. She glanced around the quaint office, her ADD mind failing to focus on any one thing.

Director Perez wasn't nearly as much of a hardass as Ogden, but he was often hard to read. The older man sat behind his large, walnut desk, studying her with a pensive expression.

Cora shifted again, trying her best to sit still, but failing as usual. Her foot was tapping a tattoo into the blue carpet.

Agent Saul Brady sat in the seat next to her, stiff-backed and attentive as ever. He didn't so much as twitch. Statuesque, he faced the director. Saul had been Cora's partner ever since she'd started at the FBI two years ago. In those short, two years, though, with his help, the two of them had made something of a name for themselves.

Their closer rate was one of the best in the office. The two of them didn't exactly resemble a likely pairing. At thirty-one, covered in tattoos and old scars, Cora's ex-military background was apparent to most at first glance. Saul, on the other hand, wore a neat suit with an equally neat, purple and gray polka-dot bowtie. He had a golden tie-clip which occasionally flashed in the light above. He had a thin brushing of pure white facial hair. Though he was only in his fifties, he didn't have a strand of dark hair remaining. He shaved his head, but when it did start to come through, it was also pale.

His neatly trimmed, pale beard perfectly framed his darker features. Saul was the definition of a poker-face. He wasn't unfamiliar with emotions, but in Cora's experience, there were few who'd mastered their inner life as much as Saul Brady.

Agent Brady didn't even glance in her direction, nor did he regard her wildly tapping foot.

Instead, he cleared his throat cautiously, allowed the proper amount of time to pass to allow the director to speak to them, but when the opportunity wasn't taken, Saul spoke himself. "Sir," he said quietly, nodding once. "As you can see, we had no choice but to enter the premises before Director Ogden arrived on scene."

Perez looked up from his computer now, adjusting the unbuttoned collar of his shirt. He let out a faint sigh, then nodded. "Right," he said. "Right, right..." He trailed off. Perez had a round face and a single curl of dark hair centered on his forehead. He'd spent a good number of years behind a desk, and the experience had added some padding to his waistline. His chair protested this with a faint creak as the director shifted to the side, one hand tapping against his keyboard.

At last, he lowered the lid of his laptop, and studied the two of them.

"According to the deputy director, he gave specific instructions for you two to wait. He received no communication in return."

Cora let out a faint little breath. She swallowed. "That was my idea, sir," she said quickly. "I was the one who wanted to scale the...er...building."

The director stared at her. "Scale?"

"Umm...oh, yeah. Didn't we mention that part?" Cora winced, shooting a quick glance at her partner.

Saul, who in her mind could only be described as a gentleman, patted her arm once in a comforting gesture, his eyes twinkling, though his impassive expression remained affixed. Then, he turned towards the director. "Sir," he said slowly. "I personally vouch for every choice Agent Shields made. I was behind her one hundred percent."

"One hundred, hmm?" said Perez. "No wiggle room there?" He paused, his expression severe, but then his round face suddenly cracked into a grin. He waved a hand, shaking his head. "I'm joking, mostly," he said, though he added this part quietly, under his breath. "I know you two do good work. And this is another example of it. Just...just next time," he said, trailing off. Then muttering to himself. He reached out absentmindedly, tapping at a small little desk toy of a metal, hovering planet. He sighed. "Who am I kidding, hmm? Next time, do exactly the same thing. Just...Maybe try not to piss Ogden off too much."

Cora felt a slow flicker of relief. The director was still smiling and nodding as he said, "Good job, you two. I mean it." He glanced at Cora, and his expression twisted into something of a look of admiration. "Scaling a fourteen-story building, huh? Shit..." He shook his head. "Good for you."

Cora winced. "It...was thirteen stories," she muttered. "Superstitious, though. So they called it fourteen..." She trailed off, hesitant. This was her least favorite part of the job.

Talking.

Talking to witnesses.

Talking to bad guys.

Talking to colleagues and co-workers.

Too much damn talking. She'd never been particularly good at it. She was seen, oftentimes, as too blunt. Or too direct. Other times, too awkward. Or her interests were deemed too unusual.

She didn't intend to be socially off-putting. And with her *own* people, ex-military types, she felt completely at ease. But with others?

It sometimes felt as if she were communicating in a foreign language.

Saul was mirroring Perez's smile now. He also glanced at her and gave an affirming nod.

She winced, and, leaning in, murmured, "Sorry for going radio silent back there. Just needed to focus a bit."

Saul's expression didn't change. He simply said, "You did what you had to. A woman's life was preserved. Well done, Shields." He winked now, nodding once, his voice rasping a bit as he leaned in his seat, adjusting his bowtie with a little sniff. "Back in my day, I might have been right up there with you."

Cora shook her head. "I don't think so. You don't look like you have the physique for it."

Saul's eyes narrowed. He clicked his tongue. "Let me have this one, Shields."

Cora twisted uncomfortably. She realized she probably shouldn't have said that last part. Damn social conventions required all types of dishonesty, though. She sighed, and shaking her head, she turned her attention back towards the director.

Perez was already lifting his computer lid again. He began to say, "Thank you, both. A few of your colleagues, I believe, are having a little celebratory round of drinks in the break room. Not technically protocol, but I'll pretend I don't know if you two want to stop by and—"

Before he could finish, though, the door to the office suddenly slammed open. The windows rattled. The motion of the flinging door sent the small desk toy off-kilter. The electro-magnet base yanked the floating metal planet out of the air, gluing it to the edge of the base plate.

Perez looked up, frowning. Saul glanced over, his motions slow, stately.

Cora, though, didn't even need to look. She could already tell the identity of the newcomer if only by his heavy breathing, stomping footsteps, and the sheer aura of indignation that swept with him into the room.

"Well?" Deputy Director Ogden snapped, his voice shaking. "Well?" he repeated with a sound of rising expectation. "So what did you decide, Anthony? Why is she still sitting here?"

Cora gave a weary little sigh, and only then did she turn to regard the new arrival.

Director Ogden looked like a politician. He had too much gel in his hair, and a dark suit that looked as if it had been designed to specifically complement his equally dark eyes. His fearsome gaze was currently levied on the director, but it took pauses if only to shoot daggers in Cora's direction.

Perez sighed. "Malcolm, why don't you wait outside—we can discuss this—"

But Deputy Ogden slammed a hand against his thigh. Cora hoped it hurt. "This troublemaker, this—this—*maverick*," he snarled, "disobeyed a direct command from a superior, putting herself, the victim, and her partner all in danger. She then proceeded to trespass, *sir,* and she shot a man in cold blood!"

"Wasn't cold blood," Cora murmured.

But Saul nudged her, giving a quick shake of his head if only to still her tongue.

But Cora had never been great at biting her tongue. There were two types of people in her experience. Those, in traffic, who would move to the side when a reckless driver was tailgating them.

And those, who on principle, refused to move, no matter how many times the speeder tried to intimidate them.

Cora was the second type. It didn't really matter that by simply merging lanes, it would solve the problem and move her out of harm's way.

What mattered was the principle of the matter. Tailgating assholes who sped up just to intimidate law-abiding drivers didn't *deserve* to have their way. Didn't *deserve* for Cora to pull to the side, letting them pass.

Then again, as she considered it...

Perhaps there were *three* types of people. The ones who pulled to the side. The ones like Cora who refused to budge. And then the speeders themselves, who felt as if the whole world was designed to cater to them and their narcissism.

12

She had a guess where she might classify Malcolm Ogden and his smarmy face.

The man was boasting a spray-on tan. His features were neither attractive nor ugly. They were the features of a face designed in a laboratory specifically to be as unoffensive as possible.

Those same, innocuous features, though, were screwed up in absolute fury.

Cora tried to keep her expression impassive, but she couldn't help the frown from curdling her features.

If she had expected her displeasure to affect Ogden in the least, she would have been dismayed. As it was, her experience with Ogden made it easy to know he didn't care a lick how she felt. In fact, the thirty-eight-year-old had it out for her. At first, Cora had thought it was because of her somewhat prickly personality. Blunt truth and frank honesty weren't exactly the most appreciated assets in the world of bureaucrats, but after a while, she realized that something else was driving the man's disdain of her.

It had been Agent Brady who had cracked it. She could always count on Saul for his ability to read people's motives. His intelligence was high, but his emotional intelligence was off the charts.

Saul had suggested that Ogden was jealous of Cora's success.

She had managed to claw her way out of a lower-class, rural town—the first in her family to attend college. To graduate. To go on and join the Navy, the SEALs. And then, two years ago, her career accelerated at a breakneck pace when she joined the FBI.

She supposed Ogden, having come from a family of wealthy lawyers, resented what she represented. The idea that someone could be self-made.

Though, of course, Cora had never thought of herself as *self*-made. There had been too many mentors, teachers, friends, companions, and colleagues who had helped her along the way.

She had once heard the expression: *if you want to go fast, go alone. If you want to go far, go together.* This was what she'd loved about her time in the Navy. And why her attitude was evergreen towards Saul.

"What are you gonna do about it, Anthony?" Deputy Director Ogden insisted, glaring at the man behind the table. He pointed a finger towards where Cora sat. "She's a liability, and you know it!"

Agent Brady now stood slowly to his feet; he adjusted his sleeves and smoothed the front of his suit. Brady was the type to respect authority, no matter what. But he was also defensive where Cora was concerned. And now, clearing his throat in that same way he had done when making room for Perez to speak, he murmured, "Apologies, sir," he said to the younger man, his eyes flashing, "but by my count, Agent Shields saved a woman's life. And this wouldn't be the first time. In two years, I can count at least seven other cases that were solved in no small part due to her own contributions." The older gentleman nodded as if punctuating the sentence, and added, "If you don't mind me saying."

And then he promptly sat back down, looking directly at Perez.

Ogden frowned at the older man. He shook his head. "There's a right way to do things, Saul. And a wrong way. You know this is much as I do. And if it wasn't for you looking the other way, sheltering her bad behavior, she would've been out of here a year ago. And you *both* know it."

Cora wasn't sure if there was anything she should add to this discussion. It felt uncomfortable, sitting there while someone railed against her as if she wasn't in the room. On the other hand, halfway up that industrial building, clinging to the concrete windowsill, she had *known* this was coming. Ogden seemed to have made it his personal life goal to get Cora fired.

Now, though, the director was shaking his head, his hands folded behind the table; he cleared his throat, and said, "Your concerns are taken under advisement, Malcolm. But I have to say, the department doesn't agree with you. In fact, the review I wrote for Cora last month," he said, glancing at her with a knowing look, "was only positive. She is an asset. An unconventional one, perhaps. But an asset nonetheless."

It was as if someone had slapped Ogden. He stared, bug-eyed at his superior, then glared at his two subordinates who were still reclining in their chairs on the blue carpet.

His eyes flashed and then, through tight teeth, the man with the spray tan said, "It's your call, sir."

With a growl, he turned on his heel and marched right back through the door. He slammed it as he left.

Director Perez massaged the bridge of his nose, muttering to himself and shaking his head.

Saul stood to his feet again, extending an arm so Cora could rise as well.

At first, when she had just started, she had found the gesture somewhat perplexing. Working on a team of special operators, the last thing she had wanted highlighted was her gender. By accepting his arm, at first, it had felt as if she had been declaring some weakness.

But over the months, she had come to realize that this was a foible of Saul's and had nothing to do with her.

It was slow going, but she was beginning to learn to allow others' eccentricities.

And so, she accepted his extended arm, hooking her elbow through his, and allowed her partner to help her to her feet. He patted her on the hand, and with a quick head bow towards Perez, the older agent said, "By your leave. We may partake in some of that aforementioned revelry."

The director was no longer smiling. He frowned towards the door where Ogden had disappeared. But then, with a quick shake of his head, as if reorienting, he glanced back at Agent Brady and Agent Shields. "Fine, fine," he said quickly. He nodded slowly. "Thank you. I'll be logging the official report tomorrow morning. If there's anything that looks out of place, you can let me know, and I'll have Ms. Clyde alter it. That's all. Thanks, you two. Good job. And Shields, make sure to stop by medical before you leave. They said you dodged them after the mission."

Cora didn't reply. She gave a sort of half nod. She had no intention of being poked and prodded at in the bureau's medical unit. Plus, she couldn't let them run blood tests—heaven forbid. Besides, she felt fine. She hadn't sustained any injuries. The only pain was in her arm, but this was from an old war wound. She doubted there was anything the medical team could do for her. No, she had her own solution for pain.

In fact, as she moved with her partner towards the door, she unhooked her arm, giving him a quick nod of gratitude, and stepping into the hall, she called over her shoulder, "I'm not going to be able to join you, Saul. I've got something, er...umm, something later."

He frowned after her. "Is everything all right?" He then glanced down the long hall, towards another office door that was closed. "Don't worry about Ogden," Saul said, shaking his head. "He won't be in the department for long. He's got a taste for governor by the age of forty. His family has the money to make sure it happens too."

Cora just nodded. She hadn't been thinking about Ogden at all. He was a very forgettable man. Like always, most of her attention was not captured by threats. Rather, her mind was focused on other, older memories. Flashes of recollection. Scents, sights, sounds.

She forced a quick smile, and as the door to the director's office closed, she murmured, "Thanks for standing up for me. But trust me, Saul, I'm good."

He blinked owlishly, perplexed, as if the comments didn't even make sense. She didn't blame him. For someone like Saul, the idea of not standing up for his partner was completely anathema.

She said, "Well, I gotta go. I've got somewhere to be. Thanks, Agent Brady."

He gave another quick nod.

She turned on her heel, waving over her shoulder as she hastened towards the stairwell. She hated elevators.

As she passed the foyer, though, she spotted a few figures standing near a breakroom. One of them called out, "Nice job, today, Cora!"

She gave a quick, hesitant smile and a nod.

A few others called out after her, mostly cheerful, relieved. They had been chasing Rike for months.

As she moved, though, something caught her eye through the glass of the breakroom.

Ogden was in there. She hesitated, regarding him. She had assumed he'd gone to his office. But no, he was standing against the back wall, speaking with someone she recognized from the technical advisory team. A computer nerd. This man, she didn't know well. He was an even newer hire than her. He had curly hair, glasses, and though perhaps it was just the company he kept, mean eyes.

She watched for a moment as Ogden leaned in, whispering something to the new tech agent.

But then this too was nothing more than a passing mirage. She picked up her pace, redirecting her attention, and moving towards the stairs.

As she moved, she felt something of a relief to have it all behind her.

At least she still had her job.

But there was another surge of sensation. A deeper longing. One that left her with a bad feeling in her stomach.

And she could only think of one cure.

She felt a surge of guilt. Her eyes narrowed. She began to hasten down the stairs as rapidly as her feet would carry her.

Not once did she look back.

CHAPTER THREE

Cora hadn't realized how late it was, but the dark sky clued her in. She sat in the front seat of her old Buick, her fingers tight on the steering wheel, her eyes fixed on the street corner ahead.

This wasn't the sort of place where women often frequented late at night.

But Cora didn't consider herself vulnerable.

Even if she had, it wouldn't have mattered.

The thirty-minute drive from headquarters had given her time to think.

She had been cranking music for most of the trip, trying to drown out the horrible curse of introspection.

Time to think for Cora was the same as purgatory for others.

But even the heavy metal blaring from her radio, while she cranked up the volume, hadn't been enough to calm her nerves.

She pulled along the street, coming to a halt next to an open alley.

Even with the windows rolled up, through the vents, she detected the faint scent of refuse.

She was shivering now.

This was the part that the others didn't see back at headquarters. This was the real reason she had left the Navy.

No one knew, not her partner, none of her colleagues, and certainly not the deputy director.

Her family?

Hell, when was the last time she'd *seen* them?

No, no one knew, and the urge was growing strong again.

She could feel her mind threatening to tear.

A deep, unspoken desire for something. Something *unnamed*. Something she couldn't place. Like a word on the tip of her tongue, but rather in the form of a flitting emotion. Some unmet need. Cora felt certain that psychiatrists and psychologists would have every type of theory where she was concerned.

But there was another urge. And this one was far more familiar. It was as if her soul was pulling in two directions. But she only knew how to give in to one of these desires. Like wrangling an oversized dog on a leash, all she could really do was hold on.

And so, she stepped on the gas, quickening up the street, towards the corner.

Through the windshield, she spotted three figures where she knew she would find them.

They wore hoods, had their hands in their pockets, their shoulders slumped, and were glancing one way and then the other.

All three sets of eyes landed on her, though, as she drew closer.

They tensed, going rigid, watching her.

She rolled down her window as she approached, swallowing slowly. She thought of Ogden, thought of what he would say if he saw her there. The final nail in the coffin for the case he had been so diligently attempting to make over the course of the last year.

And she would be handing it to him on a platter.

One of the men on the street corner leaned over, peering into the car. He scratched at a cheek covered in acne scars. He couldn't have been much older than she had been when she had first joined the Navy. "What you want, girl?" He said.

She didn't reply, but instead extended three fingers and tapped them against the frame of the door, her hand through the window.

One of the men, standing farther back and leaning against the alley, nodded once, and disappeared into the dark.

She heard sounds she couldn't quite place, and a few seconds later, he reemerged, hefting a small, brown bag.

"You know the drill," the first guy said, lowering his hand from scratching his chin.

She didn't say a word. Didn't protest. She simply reached into her pocket, pulled out a stack of bills that she had pre-counted on the way over, and extended them through the window.

The man took the money, and then waved her on.

She moved towards the second guy with the brown bag.

The third watched the scene, his hand still in his pockets, scowling. As the brown bag was handed through the window, the third guy snapped, "Wait!"

Everyone stopped. Cora glanced towards the guy.

He was frowning at her, frowning at her car.

She had unbuttoned her suit, hidden any sign of being a federal. But in her haste, her urgency, for a brief moment, she was worried she might have forgotten something.

18

But then the third man said, "You better move quick, lady, you have a tail."

He then nodded; the brown bag was dropped through the window, and all three of the young men turned, moving hastily back into the alley. Cora frowned, reaching for the bag, and feeling the familiar paper crumple under her fingers.

She glanced in the rearview mirror, frowning towards another car, which had turned onto the street.

Now, though, it was idling by the same curb where she had stopped. A tail.

Was the guy right? Or just being jumpy?

Maybe this was just another client?

But when she glanced back towards the street corner, all three of the purveyors of pharmaceutical wares had absconded.

The car parked by the curb still idled, the headlights glaring at her. A red aura from the brake lights stained the concrete.

She watched, her heart in her throat. But then the lights died, the car door opened, a figure emerged, and approached the glass door of one of the many businesses.

She felt a flicker of relief and rolled up her window. Taking the advice, she made a hasty retreat, moving back through the streets, blowing a stop sign, and turning onto the main road.

As she did, she couldn't wait. With a shaking hand, she reached for the brown bag, her heart pounding in excitement.

She had run out a couple of days ago. Two days was a long time to go without replenishing.

If not for chasing the billionaire killer, she wasn't sure she would have made it.

But as she reached into the bag and removed the nondescript bottle that rattled with pills, she felt a surge of self-loathing.

Her hand gripped the steering wheel, the other bunched around the bottle of pills in the brown bag.

Her gaze fixed on the road through the windshield, tracking every crack, crevice, and bump.

Under the cover of night, she moved quietly through the city, away from the street corner.

She opened her window more, allowing the breeze to flow through. But the cool air and the fast car did little to help distance Cora from the negative emotions now swirling in her. Not just PTSD. Not just memories of violence, torture, and wounding. Not just memories of the rescue staged by her team. The memories of another year in service, despite the pain.

But older memories too. Recollections of a best friend...

A friend closer than blood. In fact, she had *been* blood. Only a two-year age difference between them. Cora thought of her sister, her best friend at the time, and of her golden, curly hair for a brief moment—she felt another flood of pain.

Sometimes it felt as if the only thing life had to offer was pain.

Physical pain was one thing, but there were other types of agony too.

Other types of torment.

The pain of loss, in Cora's opinion was second only to the knowledge that all things lost could never be returned.

She shook her head, trying to dislodge the thoughts. But demons had a way of latching onto one shoulder. They didn't move so easily. And so, with a shaking hand, now, she unlatched the lid of the nondescript bottle, fiddling with the pills. She recognized them easily enough.

In a way, she was an expert on certain pharmaceuticals.

She avoided anything she thought would permanently damage her ability to do her job. But otherwise, she wasn't picky. Alcohol was also another favorite.

She reached towards her glove compartment, still keeping to the road, but unlatched the compartment and shifted a few papers before snatching the small, metal flask she kept there.

As her fingers skimmed the cold metal, she released a faint sigh of release.

And then, she tossed back a few pills, not counting them.

She took a long gulp of straight whiskey.

She picked up her speed, the wind tearing through the open window now and reverberating in her ears.

She swallowed the pills and took another long drink.

She leaned back, head against the cushioned headrest, eyes closed.

She smiled faintly, overwhelmed by a surge of absolute gratitude.

It took a few moments for the chemicals to have their affect. It wasn't quite the same thing as peace, but it was potent distraction. Intentional redirection.

And for someone with ADD, distraction was often as good as peace itself.

She looked into the rearview mirror, forcing a smile.

Of course, she didn't really mean the smile. Part of her had been hoping Perez would fire her. Part of her wanted the excuse. If she had been fired, at least she had an explanation for this choice. Cora felt the buzz slowly creeping along her arms, like goosebumps. A prickle along her back. She could feel her mind slowing down, could feel the slow sense of calm.

She found she could even breathe a bit easier. Her mind grew foggy as if she was staring through opaque glass.

She yawned, closing her eyes and opening them again. She reached up, slapping at her face with one hand, and stared at the abandoned roads.

She hadn't realized just how late she'd been kept at the office. Hadn't realized how late it really was. There was something soothing about the night. Something soothing about the dark.

It was as if it was designed specifically to hide her. She had spent much of her life in hiding.

And so, even half high she was able to know when someone was trying to *find* her.

She spotted the car behind her.

The headlights illuminated her vehicle. She stared into the mirror, frowning briefly.

It took her a second, blinking a few times, but then she realized it was the same car from the street corner.

Makes and models aside, she had always had a knack for remembering license plates. And now, as she stared into the rearview mirror at the car, she didn't recognize the number.

Her first instinct had been to expect the FBI. Maybe even Agent Brady.

But no, the car was a Mercedes. A new model.

She frowned towards it, and bit her lip.

And then, on a whim, she hit the brakes.

Her vehicle skidded.

She veered into the shoulder, going still, *waiting...*

A few moments passed, and the car behind her stalled. Then sped up again, as if caught in indecision.

Her eyes narrowed at the motion.

It really was following her.

She waited on the shoulder of the road, watching as the vehicle sped past her. Clearly, the driver was more focused on her than the road, as he hurtled through a red light. There was a flash as his picture was taken.

It took her a moment to think through what she wanted to do. The car raced past her instead of stopping. What did that mean?

They didn't intend harm?

They were waiting for a better shot?

She could feel her mind spinning. Could feel the same sense of guilt undercut by self-loathing.

She shook her head, feeling the prickle along her skin, the buzz intensifying.

Then, she muttered under her breath, "Think you can follow me?"

Her lip curled into a sneer.

She scowled and floored the gas. She ripped from the shoulder, buzzing the intersection. It was still too late for there to be many cars.

She turned on her brights, if only to let the car ahead know that she was coming for it.

She tore after it, the engine roaring.

Her heart was pounding wildly, her blood rushed to her cheeks. She suddenly grinned and let out a shout of exhilaration, pounding her hand against the steering wheel.

She raced up the highway, picking up speed, drawing closer to her tail.

Now, the driver seemed to realize he was being pursued.

His vehicle began to swerve, moving into the far-right lane and heading towards the ramp.

She was now honking her horn, flashing her lights—nothing more than an attempt to unnerve her pursuer.

The tires skidded, leaving rubber, but she followed, hitting her brakes and nearly spinning out. She jolted to the side, readjusted, and then hastened down the ramp following the Mercedes through an underpass, towards the bridge.

The Mercedes was struggling to outpace her; this wasn't a function of the car's ability, but rather the driver's nerves. She was nearly pushing a hundred now. And all she felt was excitement.

Suddenly, the car in front of her was honking as well. She was getting closer, closer. They were about to pass under a bridge.

She hit the bumper, a love tap, really. She nudged it, and the car in front again blared its horn in protest.

She allowed a little space, and then hit the bumper again.

Pull over, she thought.

She leaned on her own horn.

There was a chance, as she stared at the vehicle, that the Mercedes would try to outpace her.

This, she knew would be a mistake. She wasn't about to let him get away, whoever he was.

As if sensing this, or simply too scared to keep up the high-speed game of chicken, the vehicle began to slow. The tires whirred against the ground and began to go still. After a few moments, the car came to a rolling halt. She decreased her speed as well, following closely behind.

She slowly approached the stalled car, her weapon in hand, aimed towards the driver's side window. "Don't move!" she shouted. "Show me your hands!" There was no response. "Open your window and put both your hands out!" she yelled.

She moved slowly, her weapon gripped tightly; her mind was able to focus on the gun barrel, on the trigger, on the firm grip.

As she approached towards the bright lights, she blinked a few times, shaking her head.

She moved hastily forward, one foot at a time, weapon raised.

Slowly, the front window began to roll down.

She tensed, waiting, preparing to fire at a moment's provocation.

But then two pale, trembling hands were pushed out the window, the fingers spread wide.

The hands were followed by a shrill voice. "Don't shoot. I'm unarmed. Dear God, don't shoot!"

She hesitated a moment. It took her a second, but then, with a sinking sensation, she realized she recognized that voice.

A slow, cold feeling of dread began to rise within her.

She took a step to the side, getting a better view of the figure.

She found herself staring at a man with curly hair and mean eyes.

The tech agent who had been talking to director Ogden. The recent hire.

And there, sitting on the seat next to him was a camera.

It only took her a second to piece it all together. The cold lump in her throat fell into her stomach and turned to a ball of lead. "What do you think you're doing, following me?" She said, her voice shaking. Of course, she knew the reason.

He gave a quick shrug, another, and then, in the same shrill voice, he said, "N-now, now, it's no good shooting me. Even if you kill me," he gulped, "I've already sent the photos. No good!" he nodded adamantly, as if confirming his own claim.

At his words, though, she felt a shiver. "Say that again?"

He hesitated, and, in a small voice, equally shrill, said, "I said it's no good killing me. If you murder me, it won't matter. I already sent him the pictures."

"What *pictures*?" She shook her head, her mind fuzzy now.

The tech agent shifted uncomfortably, clearing his throat, blinking out at her. His expression reminded her something of a rat, with an angled nose, and a light dusting of gray fur in an attempt at a mustache. But the whiskers were just as twitchy as his disposition.

"The pictures I took of you buying on that street corner! I have it all. I have it *all*. I also have it when you were swerving back there, and," he added, stiffly, "I might add, I can smell the alcohol on your breath." He wrinkled his nose in disgust. But then, he swallowed, glancing towards the gun.

Instantly, realizing she was still pointing the weapon, she lowered it. "Director Ogden sent you?" she said.

He glanced to the side, shifting uncomfortably. Then, in a whisper as if somehow it didn't count, he murmured, "Yes, of course. I don't know what you did to piss him off, but he's been paying me well to keep an eye on you."

She stared at the man. She shook her head. She was losing her edge.

No, a small voice whispered. She wasn't losing her edge. She was giving it away. Burning it like paper every time she took those pills, took that drink.

She felt another burst of shame and humiliation.

She stared at the man behind the steering wheel, and only then, her mind moving slower than usual, did she realize the truth.

Her life was over.

Ogden was going to ruin her.

CHAPTER FOUR

The dreaded phone call came with the arrival of the sun through the blinds.

And at the same time, Cora received devastating news.

It started as a chirp. A text message on her phone. She glanced at the message, frowning. An unknown number.

She hesitated a moment, staring at the number. The area code was Colorado. Did she know anyone in Colorado?

Cora winced, staring at the phone she'd plucked off the bedside table. She took a moment, yawning as she studied the device. Her head was pounding, her mouth felt like cotton. The deep sense of shame, of regret, filled her where she lay on the bed in her apartment. The night before had all become a blur.

She could remember letting Ogden's little PI go. Could remember the horror-filled trip back to her flat in the city.

And now, she wrinkled her nose as she began to open the strange text message from Colorado. But in the middle of it, her phone began to ring.

The screen switched from white to blue, and she lifted the device, studying the incoming call.

This number she recognized.

Director Perez.

Her heart skipped a beat.

It wasn't common for the director to call her in the middle of the day.

She let out a shaking breath, swallowing back a rising bile. She closed her eyes for a moment, flopping her head back on the pillows and willing the device to go silent.

But it kept ringing, taunting her.

She let out a long sigh, her insides worming with anxiety.

And then, she slowly murmured under her breath, "I can do hard things."

It was a mantra she'd learned back in the Navy.

A sort of promise to herself.

If ever she broke that covenant, of balking once those fated words were uttered, it would ruin the magic in them completely.

I can do hard things.

It was a challenge to herself. A promise. If she didn't follow through, there was nothing left.

And so, she lifted her phone, exhaling in a flutter again, brushing her hand through the shoulder-length portion of her hair. As she hooked her hair behind her ear, she answered the phone.

"Hello?"

No greeting, no introduction. "Cora?" said Perez's voice.

Cora. Not Agent Shields, but Cora.

"I have Director Ogden with me, here, Cora..." She gave a little huff of air. "I'm sure you saw the email making the rounds..."

She hesitated, frowning. "I—no...no sir." She kept the trembling from her voice, and hastily cycled to her email client on her phone, opening it and quickly glancing through the unread messages, parsing out any retail promotions with practiced ease.

And then...She spotted it.

Untitled. Five attachments. Pictures.

She clicked the link. The email address was anonymous. Yet sent on the FBI's closed server. And as she scanned the CC list, she realized that the files had been sent to everyone at the office. She felt a lance of absolute shame, closing her eyes briefly.

Of course, she didn't need to open the attachments to recognize the photos.

But she did anyway.

And there it was, in high definition, the proof of her little demons. The first image showed her car, pulling in front of the drug-dealers from the night before. The images became a blur as her memory tried to fill in the gaps. She spotted an image where money exchanged hands. Where a brown paper bag was passed into her window.

She spotted a small video clip of her car swerving over a yellow line as she drove recklessly.

And then another image of her with a gun in hand, her bleary, red eyes glaring towards a flash of light as she wobbled forward, trying to chase down the man taking photos.

She stared at this final image.

Stared at a face she barely recognized. The high cheekbones did little to compensate for the haggard expression. The slack jaw and sloppy gait only further exaggerated her predicament. There, on her shirt collar, she thought she even spotted a stain of alcohol.

She shook her head, helplessly. She swallowed.

Ogden had sent it to *everyone*. Not just to the Director. But everyone at the office. He didn't just want her job. He wanted to humiliate her.

And he'd succeeded.

She deleted the email rapidly, and closed the app, her phone now on speaker.

"Cora?" Director Perez said, his voice firm. "Can you hear me?"

Cora swallowed faintly. She paused, closed her eyes, then murmured, "Yes, sir."

"Cora, is there an explanation for this? Those pictures..." Perez trailed off. He sounded more surprised than anything. Sad, almost. She could hear the tone of inevitability. She knew this was only going to end one of two ways.

What else could she do, anyway?

It wasn't like she could rewind time.

So, she said nothing. Part of her wanted to lie, but she'd spent a lifetime avoiding the dishonesty so many participated in. All she could do was sit there, propped in her bed, in a dark room, her head still splitting from a night of indulgence, her body in pain.

"Cora," Perez said quietly. "I'm going to ask you something. And I need you to be honest with me. From what I gather, these pictures were taken last night." He inhaled, his voice going firm now. "Has this *ever* happened before?"

Lie! Just lie!

She ignored her subconscious. What was the point, anyway? They'd drug test her. She'd be on a shit list. It didn't matter.

None of it really mattered. She lowered slowly back against her pillow, eyes wide as she stared at the ceiling. "Yes," she said simply.

"On a case?" Perez said, his voice tight.

A swallow. "Y-yes."

"Jesus Christ," Perez snapped. "Are you joking?"

"No."

"Dammit, Cora. I—I could bring you up on charges, you know that?"

"I'm...I'm very sorry, sir."

"I don't give a shit, Cora. Dammit." He trailed off, exhaling deeply. He paused, composed himself, then continued. "Obviously, you're fired. I'll be passing this along and seeing if there's anything else we're going to need to do. You'll hear from me soon." He hung up.

She could hear the disgust in the silence.

Or perhaps that was simply her own subconscious whispering. She could feel the shame, the guilt, and so she just lay there, head on a pillow, staring at the ceiling, her phone pressed against her cheek, the cold glass slowly warming. She let out a shaking breath.

It didn't even hurt.

Fired...but it felt...numb. It all felt numb.

It was only as she lifted her phone that she glanced at the text message. Half expecting it to be from a colleague, or even her partner, she was surprised, then, when she read the message.

"Are you able to make it to Addie's funeral?" A pause, then another text. *"Did you get the email?"*

She felt a cold prickle along her skin, along her face. She stared at the message.

Addie's funeral.

Addie?

Who did she know named—

And then her eyes widened. A sudden flood of horror filled her. She rapidly cycled to her email, still in the coffin of blankets and pillows. And as she scanned the email, her eyes landed on another message, from two days ago that she'd missed. It had come to her personal inbox, and during the case chasing Rike, she hadn't had much time to respond to it.

But there it was. An RSVP.

And when she clicked the link, her fears were confirmed.

"Shit..." she murmured under her breath, staring in horror at the image of a stone-faced woman with olive skin staring at a camera. She was wearing a navy uniform.

Adelaide Johnson.

She'd gone through BUDS a year ahead of Cora. They'd become fast friends as two of the only women in the unit. Her eyes quickly scanned the information beneath the RSVP. Nothing much. Just a time and a date. Colorado, later *this* evening.

She frowned at the date, glanced at her phone, and felt panicked. The funeral was today? What the hell?

She cursed again, kicking out of bed, but finding her legs were heavy, weary. She didn't even feel the energy to throw off her blankets. She just lay there in her sweatpants and t-shirt, staring at the phone.

She clicked over to the only social media platform she ever

28

checked, scrolling to her friends. She clicked the avatar for Adelaide Johnson.

And there, she spotted a post.

It started with: *This is Addie's sister. It breaks my heart to bring this news...*

It went on, but it took Cora a few tries to read—to even *process* the horrible information.

And Cora leaned back, blinking owlishly.

Addie had taken her own life last week.

Killed herself with a bottle of pills.

The sister opined further down about not knowing about the grief, the tears. And in a way, Cora's heart went out to her. But also...

Her eyes moved towards the kitchen counter, landing on her own small bottle of pills.

She'd paid a premium for those.

Her metal flask lay on the cold tiled floor, forgotten briefly, a small puddle of brown liquid having glazed one of the stones, hinting at the only remnants of the contents found in her secret stash.

It was like a one-two bunch.

A basic, straight combo that had often sent her reeling back in her fighting days. Boxing had been one of her favorite ways to train...

One. Fired.

Two. Friend dead.

And a follow up third. The funeral was today, and Cora was nothing more than a waste of space. A horrible piece of shit. A useless waste of breath.

She closed her eyes as the accusing thoughts echoed in her mind. She let out a faint rattling breath, and then pushed to her feet, shoving off the bed. She wobbled a bit, but at least managed to retain her feet.

A funeral in Colorado...later that night.

She was in West Virginia.

Did she really want to take a flight?

She groaned, flopping back onto the bed.

Just a few more minutes...

She was surprised at how empty she felt. The firing wasn't the worst part. Public humiliation didn't matter either.

The world mirroring back the contempt she already felt was only a confirmation of what she felt about herself.

The scariest part of it all, she realized, was just how much she didn't care.

About any of it.

She was so...so numb.

Scaling buildings, chasing bad guys, and shooting killers reminded her of the glory days. But now, laying on her bed, too weak to even walk towards a suitcase...she only felt numb and deeply empty.

Could she make it to a funeral? Even for a friend like Addie?

This too, she realized with a sinking sense of horror, didn't seem to matter at all.

Nothing mattered.

It all felt bleak.

"I can do hard things," she whispered at the air.

But this time, all this prompted, with a herculean effort, was for her to sit up again and stare across her small, dark, and empty apartment.

***

She tugged uncomfortably at the sleeves of her old dress uniform. A couple of the bronze buttons were missing. The dark blue creased in odd places, and she hadn't had time to get it ironed, or cleaned for that matter. It still smelled vaguely of smoke from the last time she'd worn it at a bit of a send-off bash for one of her old commanders. They'd had a bonfire and the smoke still lingered in the fabric.

Now, though, as she walked stiffly up the steps of the church, she tried not to glance to the left or to the right, ignoring the other men and women wearing black, moving around her.

Cora faced the doors to the church and resisted the urge to turn and beat a tactical retreat.

She frowned at the open doors, like the yawning mouth of a chasm. It wasn't the church, so much, that made her uncomfortable. But rather, the memories associated with the building.

She could remember brighter days in her youth. Could remember finding peace beyond doors like these. But this had been lost, like so many other things in her life.

And now she felt uncomfortable moving up the steps.

But still, Addie had been a good friend. This was the least she could do.

Cora approached a row of pews in the back of the church. Inside, the building was structured in a contradictory fashion. The facade, the windows, the old air conditioning system, and even the carpeted stage all suggested this was of humble construction. As if the building itself was boasting the lack of waste. But the pews, some of the art on the walls, and many of the attendees, looked like fine wine served in a red solo cup.

She glanced around, searching for familiar faces. There were other members from her old platoon. She spotted a few of them towards the front of the church. But far too few. Many, she knew, lost in action. Others too drunk, high, or pained to bother flying across country.

She also spotted a tall, proud man with a bristling, broom-shaped mustache. One of her old commanders.

He was the one she knew best out of those in attendance.

She promptly walked to the other side of the room, away from the commander, determined to avoid any uncomfortable conversations.

Her ears were still ringing from the phone call earlier that morning. Even now, many hours later, she couldn't quite bring herself to face the reality.

She had been fired.

Her attention moved towards the figure on the stage who was speaking into a microphone.

The woman had neat, blonde hair. Glasses perched on her nose, she wore a sleek, black suit. Her eyes were stained red, and she sniffed as she spoke into the microphone. It took Cora a moment, but she thought she recognized the woman. More accurately, she recognized that upturned, celestial nose. Those green eyes. She recognized the features of her friend. This must have been the victim's sister. Addie had shown pictures when they'd been overseas.

The woman on the stage, having gathered herself, said, "Thank you all for being here. Sorry for the late start. We wanted to give everyone who RSVPed a chance to show up." Her eyes glanced towards a section of seating that was completely abandoned. She sighed slowly, and shook her head, her blond hair swishing.

Cora also noticed the many empty seats.

Other platoon members or squad mates.

She knew, from the time she had served with these people, that it wouldn't have been out of indifference or any sort of selfishness that they had chosen not to come. Rather, she was aware of the many demons that might keep someone back.

She closed her eyes and let out a faint sigh. When she opened them again, though, as the woman up front continued to speak, she found herself distracted.

Cora glanced sharply off to the side, tracking movement.

31

Horror of horrors: a tall, straight-postured man was coming towards her.

The man had a neat, silver haircut. His eyes were blue like the sea under sunlight. He walked with a nearly perfect gait, except for a stiff left leg, which trailed behind him.

Cora had been there when Commander Grayson had received that particular injury.

She shifted uncomfortably as he moved back towards the pews she had chosen. There was no mistaking his trajectory, as his blue eyes were fixed on her.

The sister on the stage was now sharing some preliminary words. An organ played in the background, sad music as if to set the mood.

Cora looked towards the stage, exhaling slowly.

But Grayson slipped into the seat next to her, turning to face the front, and at first, he didn't say anything. He was wearing a similar uniform to hers, though his, she detected, smelled of soap rather than smoke. He had been at the bonfire, two years ago, when they had last reconvened.

"Sir," she said at last, with a stiff nod. She was trying to pay attention to what was being said from the stage, but it was becoming difficult. She didn't want to talk to anyone from her past. Didn't want to have to go through the motions. Inevitably, questions always came up. "What are you doing now? How is the work treating you? How are you?"

None of those questions had particularly satisfying answers.

Commander Grayson shifted once, standing with his arms neatly behind his back, and he glanced at her, shooting her a sidelong look. "How are you, Cora?"

Just like she'd thought—a question she didn't want to answer. She didn't want to lie. So, she just shrugged and kept her eyes focused on the stage. It was difficult too because Commander Grayson, among everyone, had been one of her favorite supervisors. In fact, he had received that injury to his left leg on a rescue mission that had helped free her and one of her team members from an enemy prison camp.

As she considered these memories, she felt a flash of images swarm across her mind.

She closed her eyes, exhaling slowly. When she opened them again, Grayson was saying, "You look rough, Cora. Tired. Have you been getting sleep?"

She exchanged a glance with the silver-haired commander. Just like

32

old times, she figured. They hadn't seen each other for nearly two years, and yet there he was, picking at her appearance and her lack of sleep. Soon, he would be asking her to do push-ups or to provide a tactical summation of her last few months. She kept her tone light, though, and simply said, "Didn't sleep super well last night, sir. How are you?"

He gave a quick shake of his head. "Can't complain, can't complain. Lisa is making burgers afterwards. A few of the others are going to pour a couple of beers on behalf of Adelaide. Would you like to join?"

Cora shifted uncomfortably. Lisa, the commander's wife, was nearly as intimidating as he was. Beautiful and pale-haired, she had survived three bouts with cancer.

Cora though, gave a noncommittal shrug. She mumbled something, unsure, even, what she was saying.

The commander glanced at her. "What was that?"

She hesitated, cleared her throat, and mumbled again.

She closed her eyes, realizing now that incoherent mutterings weren't going to suffice, and said, simply, "Maybe. I actually think I might have some plans after."

She couldn't think of anything she wanted less than to reminisce with old military buddies and reveal her recent firing from the FBI.

The commander just nodded once. "Think about it; good seeing you."

Then, giving her a long look, he reached into his pocket, pulled out a small notepad and a little pencil, like the type found in restaurants, and quickly scribbled something. He handed the note to her. "My number," he explained. "If you need anything."

He studied her a moment longer, those intimidating blue eyes seeing far more than she was comfortable with. But then, mercifully, he handed her the note and moved away, heading back towards his original seat next to the tall, pale-haired woman.

Cora slipped the note into her pocket and resumed attention towards the stage. Now, the young woman who had been speaking was replaced by an older woman. This next speaker was crying as she talked but was having a difficult time holding the mic to her lips.

The organist stopped playing in order to help the attendees hear.

There was some more sniffling from the front row, but Cora was distracted once more.

She hadn't taken anything this morning. But with all of the crying, the morbid circumstance was filling her with a slow prickle of longing—she had left home without grabbing her bottle of pills.

33

Did this place have drinks?

Shit. No, she was in a church. She'd forgotten.

And then, to make matters worse, her phone began to ring.

She winced suddenly, her hand darting rapidly to the yodeling device.

A few of the attendees glanced back at her like waves of black suits and dresses shifting on the sea.

She managed to silence the phone, and winced apologetically, but took this as an excuse to duck out of the church once more. She retreated to the steps, where some of the funeral attendees were still tardy, but making their way into the building.

As soon as she glanced at the number, though, she hung up.

She grimaced, realizing, perhaps, that her first instinct might not have been the best.

As she stared at the phone, it began to ring again. Now that the phone was on silent, she just watched it, the screen lighting up with the familiar number. Her commander was one thing, but her partner?

Agent Brady could be persistent.

Still, she didn't reply. She allowed the phone to go to voicemail.

But instead of leaving a message, Saul simply tried calling again, the phone ringing once more.

She cursed faintly, willing the device to stop. But now, by the third ring of the third call, some of her frustration took the place of shame. She answered, "What?"

Instantly, she winced. Too blunt. Too aggressive.

But though they had only been partners for two years now, Agent Brady was somewhat accustomed to Cora. He cleared his throat and said, delicately, "Agent Shields?"

She bit her lip. It wasn't *agent* anymore. But she didn't have the heart to correct him. Undoubtedly, he had already seen the email. He would have been notified by the director.

"I don't want to talk about it," she said simply. She hoped this would be it. That she would be allowed to simply hang up.

She stood leaning against the rail outside the church.

But then Saul said, "I saw the email. I wanted to tell you something."

She just maintained her silence, wishing she could just run and hide.

"I'm not angry at you, Cora. I hope you know that. I'm sad. I'm disappointed and I wish you had asked me for help."

She blinked at this.

Saul sniffed, somehow communicating poise and elegance to his voice even over the phone. "Why didn't you tell me, Cora?"

She felt the lump in her throat as he said her name—the sleep deprivation, the self-denial was getting to her. "I'm sorry?" She said faintly.

"You *should* have told me," he said quietly. "I would have been there for you; I hope you know that."

Cora bit her lip. "Saul, I appreciate it. Really, I do. But what I have, no one can help."

She felt a lance of pain along her shoulder and arm—memories tried to surface. She closed her eyes and exhaled in frustration. The organ music was crooning behind her. She could hear more sobbing.

She said, "Thank you for the call. Really. And I'm very sorry." Her voice shook. But she said, as clearly as she could, "Really, I am *very* sorry."

She allowed Saul to process what she'd said as she didn't want to hang up right away. Her partner deserved at least that much. Her *ex*-partner.

She had always liked the man, and he had been one of the few people to initially like her. In a way, she had often joked that he had helped tame her. It was a different business working with the military in the field compared to working with bureaucrats in an office.

Saul said, simply, "Don't hesitate to call, Cora. I mean that."

"Thank you, Saul," she said, feeling a jolt of affection, accompanied by grief. She sniffed, and said, "You know, I'm actually at a funeral for a friend. No one you know. Is it alright if I get back to you later?"

"Of course. I'm sorry to hear that. Was it someone close?"

"Once upon a time. But things change. I'll talk to you later, okay?"

They bid their farewells, and as she hung up, Cora wondered if this was even true. Would she ever talk to him again?

She stood leaning against the church rail; she didn't want to go back inside. She could still hear someone speaking into the microphone. The same organ music. The faint shuffles and sobs.

And then the door opened with a creak. A woman stepped out, her hands shaking so badly that she dropped the box of cigarettes she'd been carrying.

Cora instinctively reached down, snatching the box, and handing it back to the woman.

She received a quick nod and a muttered, "Thanks."

It took Cora a moment, but then she stared, recognizing the woman with the blonde hair and upturned nose. She no longer looked as nervous as she had on stage, but she certainly didn't look happy. Cora hesitated as the woman removed a cigarette. She glanced up, extending the pack towards Cora. But she shook her head, slowly stowing her phone. "You look like your sister," Cora said slowly.

The woman gave a little sigh and forced a smile, causing her left cheek to dimple.

She studied Cora, and said, "Where did you know Addie from?"

Cora adjusted the sleeves of her uniform, clearing her throat.

The woman paused, took a step back, reclining against the opposite rail outside the church, and then she gave a longer look. She nodded. "Navy?"

"We did one tour together. She was a good friend. I'm sorry to hear she died."

The woman took a puff of her cigarette, lowering her lighter and slipping it back into her pocket. She blew the smoke towards the street. "She didn't die. She killed herself. There's a difference."

Cora just watched the younger woman.

"I'm Jamie, by the way." She refrained from extending a hand in greeting.

"Cora."

"What do you do for a living, Cora?"

Another one of the hated questions. But as she stood there, facing a woman she didn't know, but who resembled one she had, Cora felt a strange sense of freedom. Answering this question honestly to a stranger came with no cost. What did it matter what Jamie thought of her?

The commander, she hadn't spoken to. Agent Brady, she hadn't wanted to speak to. But this strange, sad woman, smoking on the steps, and running a hand through her blonde hair—perhaps she was the receptacle for an admission of guilt. Cora just shook her head, glancing towards the street, and said, "I used to work at the FBI until this morning."

At this comment, though, Jamie looked up, surprised.

Cora said, "I was fired for too much drinking. Drugs."

She looked at Jamie, refusing to glance away. Perhaps it was her naturally blunt, candid personality. Perhaps it was that she had flown across country and was speaking to a stranger. In a way, outside the church, it almost felt like confession.

36

There was something more intimate and personal about this interaction than any she'd had inside that building with another person. Often, she felt as if people entered churches to meet God. And yet, it was the back of someone's head she grew most familiar with, sitting in a pew, staring towards a man attempting to guilt her into behaving better. It wasn't that Cora disliked religion. She knew many religious people she admired—Commander Grayson, being one of them—but Cora felt this was more her style: outside the church, on the stairs, talking about drugs, and watching a woman smoke.

The smoking woman gave a little chuckle, shaking her head. "Sounds like a rough day."

Cora blinked at this reaction. It wasn't the tongue lashing she had expected. She shifted uncomfortably, feeling the metal bar press into the small of her back. She glanced towards her old buddy's sister. The woman took another long draft, the tip of her cigarette glowing red.

"Honestly, you sound like Addie."

Cora glanced up, hands finding their way into her pockets.

Jamie nodded. "She had a problem with drinking too." The cigarette waved in the air, back and forth, sending a few flecks of ash fluttering on the breeze beneath the gray skies. "Addie had her own demons..." Jamie snorted, shifting. "Do you want to hear something funny?"

The scent of the cigarette had now reached Cora. She inhaled slowly, the odor stinging her nostrils. "What?"

"Addie killed herself because of what happened to her daughter."

Cora frowned now. "What do you mean?"

"Not everyone knew it, but she had Caitlin young—her daughter just turned eighteen a few months ago. She was hanging with some of the wrong sorts. Coming home at strange hours." Jamie shrugged, shaking her head. "We thought it was the usual stuff. Addie would come, complaining about it, but I told her it was all going to be okay." A note of bitterness crept into her voice.

"Then she disappeared."

Cora felt a prickle along her spine. "What do you mean?"

"Exactly that. She disappeared. Was kidnapped, we think. We haven't seen her in months. And when Addie reported it to the police, the investigators looked at it and closed the case in a day. Said that because of the people she was hanging around, she was probably just a runaway. But none of the people she spent time with had seen her. One of them said they saw her being forced into the back of a car, but she was too high to remember anything." Jamie shook her head, the

37

bitterness having returned to her voice.

Cora frowned now, interjecting, "Wait a moment," she said. "Her daughter was kidnapped? How come I didn't know Addie had a daughter?"

"She didn't want anyone to know. She was embarrassed. She had Caitlin when she was only fifteen; our mom took care of her for the years she was off in the navy; it wasn't an easy life, but we had a good life," Jamie said, taking another long pull from the cigarette, and closing her eyes in grief. Her voice shook as she sighed. "I'm sorry I don't mean to—it's just..." she trailed off, tapping one pale finger against the side of the cigarette, and watching as ash fluttered. Then she looked up, and her gaze was attentive, piercing. "So, you work for the FBI?"

Cora frowned. "I used to. I don't anymore."

But Jamie said, "I understand, but you would still have connections, right?"

"What are you getting at?" Something about the tone of the conversation seemed to have shifted. Cora felt prickles along her skin.

"I'm not getting at anything...I'm begging...my niece was kidnapped. My sister is dead and there's nothing I can do about it. But someone like you..." She trailed off, shrugging once.

Cora studied the woman; she felt a strange shiver along the backs of her hands. In part, because when she looked at this young woman, heard the grief in her voice, Cora couldn't help thinking of her own life. There had been so many parallels between her and Addie. They had hit it off right away, but there were parallels after her death too.

The feeling of helplessness. Of pain. Feeling trapped. Of wanting it all to end. Cora felt a shiver along her back. She exhaled briefly, trying to calm her nerves. "I don't know what you think I can do for you," she said carefully. Cora couldn't look at Jamie now, feeling a prickle of guilt that started as a knot in her stomach and spread in sharp pangs. She wanted to help. Every part of her wanted to help. But she knew that if she agreed to, there was nothing she could do officially. She'd been fired. The director had been clear; there were still discussions about pressing charges.

She'd openly admitted to being drunk on cases in the past. There was photographic evidence of her purchasing illicit drugs. She hadn't denied it.

She closed her eyes and massaged the bridge of her nose. "I can't help you," she said, and the knot in her stomach only intensified.

38

Jamie's voice was pleading now, "I'm not saying you have to do anything crazy. But you've got to have some connections. Someone who can take a second look. The police station wouldn't even take my calls. The detective in charge said it was open and shut, and he only spent the day looking at the information." Jamie had dropped her cigarette now and was waving a finger around like a conductor's baton. Her voice was increasing in volume, clearly growing agitated. "I can pay you!" Jamie said hurriedly. "Not much. But I *can* pay."

Cora winced, shaking her head. "It's not about the money. I just don't see how I can help you."

Jamie frowned, pulling another cigarette. "Fine, I get it," she sighed slowly. "Would you at least think about it?"

Cora hesitated. She didn't want to lead the woman on. As sincere as she sounded, and as much as Cora wanted to help, there was nothing she could do. She wasn't an agent anymore.

"I believe my niece is still alive," Jamie said, her voice shaking. "But no one's listening—no one is willing to help. Please," she said one more time, her fingers shaking so badly that she failed to light the new cigarette.

Cora didn't reply; the organ music had stopped now. The voices had quieted. A few people, she spotted through the open doors, were shuffling by, passing the closed casket.

Cora, again, felt that it was fitting she stay back, watching from a distance. So much of life had felt like a spectator sport. She bit her lower lip and exhaled. She wanted to say no. Wanted to give a firm reply cutting off any further request.

She was fighting her own demons, after all.

"There's no one else," Jamie said in a small, sad voice. "No one."

Still, even though Cora began to refuse, what came out instead was a question. "Where was your sister living when her daughter was taken?"

Jamie perked up, her eyes widening. She kept her tone cool, though, as she said, "Here, near the Rockies. All of our families lived in the same, small town of Westville; it's not far from here."

Cora frowned. "And it was the police in Westville who refused to investigate?"

Like a drowning victim reaching for a lifeline, Jamie spoke urgently, nodding her head rapidly in frantic motions. "Yes, exactly!" she exclaimed. "They didn't even try. Something is off about the whole thing."

Cora could feel an urge threatening to return; all she really wanted to do was get on a plane, head home, pop a few pills, and wait to hear if the FBI was going to press charges.

But in the SEALs, one of the major benefits had been the discipline they'd taught. The ability to do difficult and hard things.

What was another day? It wasn't like she had anywhere to be.

And most of all, though she hated to say it, didn't want to admit it to anyone, least of all herself, she wasn't sure what she might do if she spent the night alone, in her small apartment, drinking.

What had happened to Addie? The demons that had been chasing her since their time together overseas finally caught up.

Despair wasn't a friend to anyone, but it was a particularly deadly enemy to those who already battled on multiple fronts.

Cora wasn't sure she could take much more.

She said, her voice shaking, "Maybe I can stay another day. *Just one day.*"

As she spoke, Jamie's eyes widened.

The woman let out a little squeal of delight and took a couple of steps forward as if to hug Cora.

But the disgraced FBI agent held up a hand and shook her head. "I'm not promising anything. You have to come to terms with the fact that it may really be the case that she was just a runaway. The police might be right."

"But you'll look into it?"

Cora sighed, unsure how she had come from wanting to refuse to now giving this small concession. But then again, it really was only one day. What was the worst that could happen in a day?

"One thing, you don't happen to have a place for me to stay, do you? I'm also going to need to borrow a car."

Jamie, still excited, was nodding quickly. "Mom never drives the van. And you can stay in the living room at my place. It's cozy, but clean."

Cora nodded. "Cozy and clean will do just fine. I'll only be here for the one day. I mean it."

Jamie was nodding along, too excited to pay much attention to this admonishment.

Cora closed her eyes for a moment, wondering if she ought to change her mind. But nothing was waiting for her back in West Virginia. And besides, maybe just maybe, the police had missed something. Even though she had sometimes been drunk or high on the job, she'd also been good at what she did. She wouldn't have the same backup, or resources, or access to even the simplest of databases, but instincts and willful stubbornness were capable of going places that an amalgam of resources weren't.

She turned, walking down the stairs towards the street. Over her shoulder, she said, "I'll be back in a bit, if you don't mind giving me a ride. I have something to take care of."

Really, this was just code for, *I don't want to speak with anyone who recognizes me.*

As she moved away from the small church, hands jammed deep into her pockets, she hunched her shoulders, the shaved portion of her head feeling chilly from a faint breeze.

She wasn't sure what she had just gotten herself into; she had never confronted a police station before. Never had to double check someone else's work. But if a girl's life was on the line, she guessed it was the least she could do.

CHAPTER FIVE

Caitlin shivered, her breath coming in rapid and wild gasps. The tremble along her arms, hands, and the backs of her legs had nothing to do with the weather and everything to do with the prickle of terror.

Her shoulder bumped against metal. Her back scraped against the corrugated plastic floor of the jeep.

They had thrown her in the back, and she could feel her arm brushing against another soft limb. The young woman next to her was crying.

But Caitlin had already shed her tears; the blindfold was damp from both perspiration and her panicked weeping.

But now, after nearly an hour, she could feel the fibers of rope. Small, broken pieces of plastic flooring she had managed to puncture with her fingers had exacted a toll in pain. Blood dripped from her fingers and sharp jolts of discomfort shot up her hands even as she worked at the ropes.

But even so, she continued frantically. Rubbing back and forth, fraying ropes falling. Fibers and strands tumbling.

She felt fear like never before. The harsh, male voices from the front of the Jeep were shouting something in a language she didn't understand. Suddenly, her body jolted, and she realized they had come to a stop.

She could smell a verdant, lush breeze. Fresh air, like that of a forest, but different somehow. Strange scents and fragrances arose. The odor of cheap cologne and stale cigarette smoke wafted back from the front, competing with the other inferences.

She could feel the ropes falling, and then, the front door slammed just in time to mask her own gasp of surprise.

The bonds broke completely; her hands were free.

She resisted the urge to congratulate herself, to remove her blindfold. Right now, she had to be careful and quiet.

Her mother had been adamant that she needed to keep her cool in situations like these.

Caitlin missed her mother. Things had been rough between them for

42

years. She resented the first fifteen years of her life, being raised by her grandmother.

The last three years, her mother had returned from service.

Now, Caitlin wished she had done it all differently.

She heard more sharp voices. A sudden flare across her blindfold of bright lights. And then, a horrible sound. A gunshot.

The girl next to her let out a faint gasp, and Caitlin took this as her chance to tug at her blindfold, doing her best not to move too much.

She left it skewed over her face, peering over the edge.

She stared out, her eyes scanning, and she realized, startled, that they were in some type of jungle. The leaves above were not oak or fir. They were large, like elephant ears.

She heard other sounds coming from the dark jungle. The night was illuminated by headlights from multiple vehicles. Their Jeep, by the looks of things, though she kept her head down as she scanned, was at the back of a convoy of four cars. The car in the front had pulled off to the side of the road, and two men with red bandannas, guns slung over their shoulders, were desperately trying to move toppled branches.

A few other men, standing near the Jeep she was in, were being beckoned forward by a man who barked in an authoritative voice. He was pointing at something, and the men with guns moved away from her Jeep.

Her heart pounded. She felt a sudden surge of adrenaline. Now or never.

She tore the blindfold down and began to rise.

But just then, there was a flash of headlights. A car pulling up behind them. More angry shouting.

"What are you doing?" came a small voice next to her. It was a relief to hear English.

But Caitlin didn't reply. She paused, peering towards the glaring lights behind her. Then towards the woman at her side, who was crying.

Caitlin bit her lip. She couldn't just leave the woman here, could she?

But if she didn't, they were both as good as dead. She had heard stories of how things like this ended.

Her hair stuck to her skin, sweat slicked.

She glanced at the woman who was blindfolded and bound next her. She spotted caramel skin, and rich curls behind her blindfold.

Then, with a huff of frustration, she dropped back and pulled the blindfold over her eyes once more, as much as it pained her to do it.

She hid the ropes in the gap under the cracked plastic. And then pressed her hands in front of her, as if they were still bound.

She lay down on the plastic ground next to her fellow captive. "Stay quiet," she whispered. "It looks like something is blocking the road."

But the young woman was crying again. "What are they going to do with us?" She asked through a sob.

"Nothing nice," Caitlin said, finding her own voice shaking. But in moments like these, she channeled her mother or, at least, she tried to. As different as they were, and as many difficulties as they had faced, she had always respected her mother, the woman who had shown more courage than most people she'd ever known.

She couldn't wait to get out of here and tell her mom just how much she meant to her. It had been weeks, maybe longer since they'd seen each other.

Caitlin shivered, remembering the last time she'd been in town.

"Please, *please*, let me go."

The girl next to her was crying, her voice rising in volume. Caitlin winced. The last thing she needed was attention. She hissed sharply, "Quiet! Keep it down!"

But the young woman with the dark hair was shaking her head, voice cracking. There was the sound of thumping boots, more slamming doors. And then the engine roared to life. Someone barked something contemptuously, and there was a hand that slapped at Caitlin, coming from the direction of the front of the Jeep.

They said something again, in a language she didn't know. But then, in English, heavily accented, the same voice snapped, "Shut up!"

This only caused Caitlin's fellow captive to cry harder.

Caitlin reached out suddenly, wincing as she did, and hoping that no one noticed her free hand. It took her a second to find the young woman's arm. But then she held the woman's wrist, and gave it a quick, comforting squeeze. She whispered softly, "It's going to be okay."

This, of course, was a lie. Another thing her mother had taught her. Lying to keep someone from being scared. Lies like, I'll be there for your birthday. Or I'll see you next year. Or don't worry, I'll come home. Lies that she had believed as a child. But now, as a woman, she knew far better than to expect a happy ending.

But that didn't stop her from utilizing the same tactic. She kept her hand gripping the young woman's shaking arm.

The girl seemed to quiet. The angry voices returned to a more regular volume and then the jeep grumbled back to life; they were moving once more.

Her hands were free, but Caitlin realized, with dawning dread, she may have just missed her only opportunity to escape.

CHAPTER SIX

Cora tugged uncomfortably at the sweater she had borrowed from Jamie.

Her hair was still somewhat damp from the shower, and her back ached from that horrible, hard chair of the minivan she'd been allowed to borrow. But her belly was full, following a pulled pork and potatoes dinner after the wake with Jamie and her mother.

Now, she faced the small Westville police station.

As she moved up the parking lot, studying the place, she realized just how small the station was. Only the size of a two-story townhouse. With, by her count, two cars in the parking lot.

Westville wasn't a particularly large town. When Jamie had agreed to bring her home, and allow her to sleep on the couch, Cora wasn't sure what she had been expecting. But the place felt more rural than anything. The Colorado Rockies stood out in the town's backyard, a permanent postcard over the fenced in acreage.

On the drive to the police station, she had spotted a small library and even a public pool. But beyond that, there had only been one restaurant, and the grocery store was not one she recognized. No auto shop and no hospital. Though, she had spotted a veterinarian.

A small town, with a green sign leading in that posted a population of 900.

In a place this small, one outsider stood out like a sore thumb.

In part, that was why she had asked to borrow a sweater. Jamie was a size larger than Cora, but it was better than walking into a police station wearing her old, smoke smelling Navy uniform, and instantly standing out as an object of suspicion.

She took the stairs leading up to the police station's sliding doors.

Perhaps it was big city living, but she was surprised when the glass doors didn't slide open automatically.

She reached out with the back of her hand, pushing the door open, and stepped into the police station.

A small bell rang overhead, as if she had entered a grocery store.

A couple of men sitting behind a desk, and another behind the counter, glanced in her direction.

She could hear an angry voice in the back of the office, coming through an open door. She couldn't quite make out what the voice was angry *about*, but the volume was only increasing the closer she got the desk.

"Can I help you?" said the man behind the desk.

He was handsome, but a good ten years older than her. He was frowning too, his uniform unbuttoned at the top. He had a small white, porcelain cup. A coffee mug but judging by the smell that accosted her as she leaned forward, the contents were a bit stronger than caffeine.

She tried to focus. Shaking her head, she said, "My name is Cora Shields. I was wondering if I could speak to the person in charge of Caitlin Johnson's case."

The man tapped a ballpoint pen against a piece of paper, and leaned back, his chair creaking from the motion. "The Johnson case? Not sure I know that one."

The other man in the room, who was standing behind the counter, hadn't taken his eyes off Cora since she had entered. When she looked over, he smiled politely enough and nodded, a schoolboy face with a good-natured grin. But when she looked away and tracked him out of the corner of her eye, he stared at her like a wolf examining a hunk of meat.

She was accustomed to men like this in positions like this. But though she was used to it, she was never comfortable with it.

Still, the man with the schoolboy face said, "You remember Caitlin Johnson, Marv. That girl who ran away."

The man with the pen continued tapping; he nodded, reaching up absentmindedly with a free hand to button his collar. "That's right, I do remember," he said slowly. "Shame that. I heard that her mother just killed herself. Is that true?"

He was still watching Cora, but by the tone and tilt of his voice, he was directing the question towards the man behind him.

"That's what I heard. Sad thing, that. A fine piece like that?"

Cora looked at the second man now. He flashed another, pleasant smile, and nodded politely at her.

She frowned back. "Who was in charge of Caitlin's case?"

The handsome cop shook his head. "Can't say I know exactly. We're night shift. Our dad," he hesitated, coughed, then said, "I mean the captain...he's the one who assigns cases. I can go ask him. But by the sound of things, he's a bit busy. Maybe you should come back later."

47

Cora glanced around, spotted a bench by the door, approached it, and sat down. As she walked, she could feel the gaze of both men on her. And when she turned, the schoolboy was smiling, and the handsome one scowling

"I think I'll wait," Cora said simply.

Now, the smile fell. The scowl intensified; they shared a look, but not with her. She was beginning to get the sense that not much would be shared with her. Still, she had promised Jamie to check it out. So here she was. Checking. It. Out.

"I'm not sure what you think we can do for you," said the man with the pen. He stood up, having buttoned his collar, and frowning. "The captain is out after this; his shift is up. Maybe if you schedule an appointment, sometime next week, we can accommodate your request. Who are you, by the way?"

"Cora—"

"No, I heard your name. I mean *who* are you. I don't recognize you. Around these parts, I recognize most folk. Are you from out of town?"

Cora hesitated but saw no harm in telling the truth. She nodded once. "I'm here for the funeral of Caitlin's mother. She was a friend of mine."

The frowning man said, "Military?"

Cora replied, stiffly, "SEALs."

The schoolboy chuckled as if she had told a joke. But when she frowned at him, he crossed his arms, eyebrows going up and teasing the fringe of his reddish hair. "Holy shit, you're not joking. Man, they're letting all sorts in these days, aren't they? Not to be rude or nothing. Good for you, honey."

Cora wanted to bite her tongue; she knew that would have been what Saul would do. How often had he tried to speak to her about keeping her temper in check? But sometimes, she found it hard not to simply speak her mind. She also found it difficult to act like Saul when he wasn't around.

She felt the pain of realization that she might never see her old partner again.

Now, though, her eyes narrowing, her tone hard, she said, "You've been eyeing me since I came in here, and I'm aware that both of you are armed, and both of you are law enforcement. And you can make my life miserable if you want to, but I'm going to have to be polite and clear about this. If you don't stop insulting me, and examining me when you think I'm not looking, I'm going to come across that desk and stick my fingers in both those eyes, is that clear?"

When she finished, she tried not to wince. It had come out harsher than she had intended. Sometimes, when she started a sentence, she entered it with the best of intentions, but halfway through, she got drunk on the words themselves, and it got away from her.

And now, both men were frowning at her.

The schoolboy with the reddish hair was resting his hand on his holster. "What did you say to me, girl?"

Though, by the look of him, he was a few years younger than she was.

She didn't look away, nor did she apologize. She had said it, and so she was going to stand by it.

The other man, though, gave a quick shake of his head. "Let it go Hurley. Look, Ms. Shields, we appreciate you coming in here. And I apologize for any breach in decorum my little brother may have caused you, but, if I'm honest, maybe it's best if you schedule something and come back later."

Before Cora could reply, though, the one named Hurley was shaking his head. "Hang on. It's not all right. Did you hear her? She threatened a police officer."

Cora, again, didn't say anything. Once the words were done with, sometimes all that remained was to let the scenario play out.

She knew she was probably pushing things a bit too far. On the other hand, she had never been a big fan of law enforcement officers like this. Soft men with positions daddy had provided for them.

The boy with the reddish hair, who couldn't have been much passed his mid-twenties, was glaring at her, his hand resting ominously on his gun.

She remained sitting on the bench.

Reaching a sudden decision, the schoolboy suddenly stepped behind the desk, and began to march towards her, his shoes clicking against the tile floor.

She didn't move. Rather, she just watched him approach. If he tried to lay a hand on her, she wasn't sure what she would do. People like her old partner entered most situations with a plan.

Cora, on the other hand, felt she spent most of her life trying to figure it out as she went.

"Hang on, Hurley," said the older brother, frowning. "Let it go. You *were* staring at her. I saw you."

Hurley looked over, scowling. His face was turning the same color as his hair. "I was not," he snapped.

"You were too. And if you make me, I'll go get Dad."

The younger police officer muttered, shook his head, and sneered. "Whatever, man," he snapped.

Deciding the older brother was the more reasonable of the two, Cora looked at him. "I need to speak with whoever was in charge of Caitlin's case.

The second officer sighed, moving from behind his desk, and crossing his arms as he leaned against the piece of furniture.

"Look," he said slowly, "I'm guessing you're here on behalf of Jamie, is that right?"

Cora paused. "You know Jamie?"

"Oh, we *know* Jamie," said Hurley, the same creepy look in his eyes, somehow now reaching the tone of his voice.

Cora ignored him.

The other cop said, "She's come by a few times. Clearly very upset. She is aggrieved. I think that's the word, right?"

Cora didn't respond.

He continued regardless, "Suffice it to say, we've already looked into things. Dad was very clear. But we talked to some kids. They are confident Caitlin is off somewhere with her boyfriend. They saw her get into a car with him. Besides, I'm sure you know this, but things were not good between Caitlin and her family. Sometimes, a girl has gotta sow her oats for a bit. I'm sure she'll be back in a couple of months or something."

Cora shook her head. "It's already been a couple of months. From what I heard, someone saw Caitlin being forced into the back of a car."

"No ma'am. That was the initial statement, but it was from an unreliable witness. They were inebriated at the time. The others confirm the story. In fact, my own nephew was there. He says otherwise."

Cora glanced around incredulously. "Your nephew? Let me get this straight, you two are the officers on staff. Your dad is in charge. And your nephew is now the star witness?"

The handsome cop frowned. "Not quite sure what you're insinuating, ma'am. But let's just say this. Caitlin isn't the only young woman to pull a stunt like this. We've had two other runaways this year. They left notes, one of them left a video. They went off to Denver. Big dreams and all that. One of them said something about trying to make it to Hollywood." He shrugged and gave a little shake of his head. "This

50

shit is contagious entitlement. That's all."

But Cora leaned in now, pushing slowly off the bench. "Other young women have gone missing?"

"It's not like that. One of the kids, Cynthia Whitehall, she was a friend of the family. She was always talking about being a movie star. And so, she went off. Her mother cried for a week, but she got a voicemail just last month.

"Things are rough when kids leave the nest. But it's nothing more than that. It's a small town up here in Westville. Some people just don't like sticking around."

Cora listened to all of this, frowning now. At first, she had thought Jamie was engaged in wish fulfillment. But now, listening to this, she wasn't nearly so sure.

The offhand way the police officer was dismissing the disappearance of three girls, two of them, having somehow left video or audio farewells notwithstanding was off-putting.

"Cynthia Whitehall contacted her mother last month? And when did she go missing?"

"She left," said the man, emphasizing the last word, "about six months ago. That's all. Young women are flighty like that. Now, I really must insist, why don't you come back later. Maybe in a few days; does that work?"

Cora hesitated, but then she nodded once. "I'll call to schedule an appointment."

Before she could say anything else and get herself in trouble, she turned, moving back towards the door.

Again, she was caught off guard as it didn't open automatically. As she pushed out into the parking lot, approaching the minivan she'd been loaned, she couldn't help but scowl.

Even as she walked to the car, she could feel eyes watching her.

Perhaps it was just because it was night. The darkness affecting her. Or perhaps it was because of how those two police officers were acting.

But something was strange in Westville

She had agreed to stay a day. She had wanted to do it out of courtesy for Jamie and her sister.

But now, something else was taking root.

A bone deep suspicion.

Cora scowled, opened the front door to the van, slipped inside, and gunned the engine.

Before she had even left the parking lot, her phone was in her hand, the call connecting to Jamie, who answered on the second ring.

Before she could breathlessly greet her, Cora interrupted and said, "Do you know the address for Cynthia Whitehall's family? I need it. Right now."

CHAPTER SEVEN

Night had fallen completely. Cora stared towards the small, single-story house set on half an acre, against a backdrop of mountain peaks. Her hands twisted on the steering wheel, attempting to find some warmth in the sudden chill of the night.

She checked her phone, making sure she had the right address, and her eyes bounced from the text on the device to the number over the door.

She pushed from her car, hands in her pockets, moving towards the small home.

Cynthia Whitehall had been taken six months ago. Another runaway according to the police department.

But three girls in a year, running away from the same small town? The police writing it off as quickly as they had?

She frowned, shaking her head in frustration as she approached the house.

She tried to adopt as nonthreatening an expression as she could. A smile was too much, and so she settled for a quizzical look. Her hand raised, she knocked on the door. And then she stood awkwardly on the porch, waiting.

There was no response at first. Only the quiet. And then, she heard the sound of footsteps.

Hurried steps, with rapid and excited energy.

Another voice came from inside the house, deeper in. "Sasha, don't. Wait for me!"

But the footsteps didn't stop. Cora heard the sound of a bolt sliding, the door opening. And then, she had to glance down to meet the wide eyes of a small face. A young girl, no older than six, with caramel skin, and a wrinkled nose stared out at her. Cora stood in the door, staring down child. She cleared her throat hesitantly, eyes bouncing over springing curls, and moving in the direction of another figure stalking swiftly towards them, a bathrobe being tightened.

"Sasha, what did I say? Get away from there."

The little girl stared at Cora, a look of disappointment clouding her

53

features. "You're not Cynthia."

Cora grimaced, realizing that, perhaps, by knocking on the door so late at night, she had aroused hopes that would now only be painful. She gave a small, sad shake of her head. "Sorry, I'm not. You're right."

The little girl bit her lip, and turned, darting back to hide behind the older woman's leg. "Who are you?" said the woman in the bathrobe. She had bags under her eyes, and close-cut hair. Her face was haggard with wrinkles around her eyes. She looked exhausted, but it wasn't the sort of exhaustion that came from a lack of sleep, more like an emotional toll visible in every glint and glimmer of her eyes. And the same, dark eyes were fixated on Cora, watching her with suspicion.

"Mrs. Whitehall?" Cora guessed.

"That's right. And who are you?"

Cora extended a hand as if in greeting, but then, when she received no reciprocation, she lowered her arm. "Cora Shields. I am a friend of Jamie Johnson."

Everyone in this town seemed to know each other. The woman nodded hesitantly. "Nice to meet you. I'm sorry about Adelaide. I'm guessing you were in town for the funeral."

"That's right. Look, I know it's late. And I don't mean to be a bother but I'm actually looking into the disappearance of Adelaide's daughter Caitlin."

A look of pain flashed across the older woman's face. The expression of exhaustion morphed into one of grief.

She said, softly, "Do you think it has something to do with my daughter? Is that why you're at my door?"

"I don't know. I'm just looking into it, is all."

"Are you some sort of private investigator?"

Cora wrinkled her nose at the question; she wasn't sure why, but this comment made her uncomfortable.

"Nothing like that. Just a concerned friend. I stopped by the police station. A couple of the officers mentioned that your daughter went missing as well. I know it's probably painful to talk about, but do you mind if I ask some questions?"

Mrs. Whitehall hesitated. She glanced towards the small girl clinging to her waist. She patted those bouncy curls and whispered, "Sasha, why don't you go back upstairs?"

The little girl didn't let go at first, and the woman had to pry her fingers off one at a time, disentangling them from her bathrobe. Then, she gave a gentle little push, sending the girl gliding towards the stairs.

54

Her footsteps thumped against the wooden steps, and she disappeared at the top.

Whitehall turned back, her voice shaking. "The police said Cynthia ran away. And I understand why they thought that. My daughter was going through a rough time. We weren't exactly close..." the woman trailed off, shaking her head. Her voice shook with grief. But then she looked at Cora again and frowned. "I'm sorry, I don't know you. What do you think this has to do with Caitlin?"

"I really don't know," Cora replied honestly. "But I heard another girl went missing too."

"Erin. She was a friend of Caitlin and Cynthia. They all knew each other from school. Everyone in the town knows each other."

Cora nodded, hesitating briefly. "Was there anything suspicious surrounding the disappearance of your daughter? Anything you can tell me?"

"Nothing really. Just that we had a strained relationship. She was dating someone who I didn't know. She didn't want to introduce me. Said I was too judgmental." Mrs. Whitehall scowled, her eyes flashing at the recollected accusation.

"I see. And you say she was a friend of Caitlin's? And this girl, Erin. Who is she?"

"She also comes from a single mother family," Whitehall said with a defiant tilt of her chin. "In fact, things were rough between her and her mother too. It's a phase. They all go through it."

Cora was frowning now, though. This was the third missing girl who had a strained relationship with a single mother. And two of the girls, by the sounds of things, were dating some mysterious boyfriend.

Cora considered this for a moment. "Did you tell all of this to the police? Did the captain know?"

"It's not a very big police department. But they said she ran away. Said they had proof. I don't think they looked into it too much." The bitterness was evident in the woman's voice. But she shrugged, and murmured, "Maybe I could have been better. God, I know I could've been. But I've been trying my best. I really have." Her voice cracked, and she glanced up the stairs. She bit her lip, and looked back at Cora with those exhausted, worn features. The emotions gouged into every wrinkle.

"You're doing great," Cora said, unsure what else to add. She wasn't sure why she said it; it didn't feel as if it was her place. But someone had to, besides, her heart went out to Mrs. Whitehall—no one deserves to lose a daughter, runaway or otherwise.

"Is there anything else you can think of? Anything that stood out around the time of her disappearance?"

"Disappearance? So, you don't think she ran away?" There was a note of fear.

Cora quickly backtracked. "I don't know anything. I'm just trying to cover my bases."

Whitehall murmured something and adjusted her bathrobe. "The police were confident. You should probably talk to them. She ran away. She must've." The woman nodded her head fiercely. Clearly, she wasn't leaving room for any further discussion.

Cora supposed she would have to get answers the hard way.

CHAPTER EIGHT

Cora sat in her vehicle, staring towards the police station. She waited, sleep attempting to draw her attention to just how comfortable the back seat looked. But she had gone days without sleep in the past. She had spent nights in cold water. A little bit of exhaustion was nothing; it was a simple issue of mind over matter.

She watched the silhouette move from the glass door, the sound of jangling keys just audible on the night. Cora's own headlights were off. She had parked across the street, hidden where she ducked low, keeping out of sight.

A tall figure she didn't recognize, with silver hair and a stately beard like that of a Confederate general, approached the lone vehicle remaining in the parking lot. The man slipped into the car, pulled out of the drive, and moved onto the road. His lights flashed as he sped by, but he didn't slow, giving no sign that he had spotted her.

Cora waited, counting to ten and then, slowly, she slipped from her car, approaching the police station.

Of course, it was risky. What had started as a desire to gather some information, to check into a basic runaway case for a friend, was starting to feel *more...*

She hastened towards the police station. Cora couldn't remember having ever broken into a station before. But without credentials, and with the clear hostility from the officers, she had decided to make an audible. The dismissive way in which the department handled the disappearance of the three local girls suggested to her that perhaps they were not the most reliable source of information. Instead of asking for a report, secondhand, she wanted to look at the files themselves. Had the police even investigated the disappearances?

Worse still, a thought accompanying a shiver, were they somehow involved?

She picked up the pace, her feet skipping across the gravel parking lot. A couple of stones skittered away. She winced at the sound, compensating by breathing slowly. No one was watching. There were no security cameras outside the police station either. Either it was such

57

a small town that they didn't see the need or perhaps they didn't have the budget.

Or, possibly, the police didn't want a record of what went on behind those doors.

She was growing paranoid, and she realized perhaps her own experience with Deputy Director Ogden was impactful.

She tried not to project her disdain for that man on to anyone in Westville. But it was difficult. Especially following what seemed like neglect on three separate cases.

Regardless, she needed to look at those files.

She didn't approach the front door, though. She had seen the man lock it. And besides, if anyone was going to drive by, she would be in full view.

But infiltration was part of her training. Part of what she knew best.

Not that it took a genius to move around the side of the building, already scanning for lower windows, grates, cellar doors. Anything.

What she found was a rear-facing window with rusted, metal bars.

One of the bars, she noticed, was loose from its fixture, having rusted completely through.

She glanced out of the alley, the faint scent of mildew and mold lingering, coming from what looked like a smashed wardrobe turned into wet kindling.

There was a burst of bright lights, and she froze. A car passed by, disappearing.

She began to move, picking up the pace.

She grabbed hold of the rusted bar, flakes of red tumbling, and she began to jerk it back; Cora pulled at the metal bar, her teeth pressed tightly together from the exertion. More red flakes fell, and the bar bent slowly upwards. The weathered, rusted spoke turned outwards and then *snapped*.

The weathered worn, half-eaten portion at the top came clean away, and she had to snatch the bar before it hit the ground.

She winced, gripping the metal, feeling a sudden shiver. Cora frowned as she lowered the metal bar onto the ground, and then faced the window. It was perhaps too much to hope that it had been left unlatched. And after a few attempts at trying to push it open, she gave up. She bent over, snatching the metal bar again. She took off the sweater she had borrowed, bracing it against the window. The cool, nighttime Colorado air assuaged her tattooed skin. Her muscles tensed as she aimed with the metal bar, shot a glance towards the alley, and then swung.

There was a quiet *thump*. Nothing happened. The glass was thicker than she had anticipated.

She frowned, took a step back, her sweater wedged against the other bars, still braced against the glass, and she swung again.

This time, the glass smashed. It shattered, tumbling onto her sweater inside the room beyond.

She winced against the sound. A couple of pieces of glass, caught on the fabric of the sweater, tumbled into the alley, making a sound like snapping fingers.

Tense now, she waited, listening. But there were no alarms, no shouting. She supposed it made sense that the tiny police station with no security camera also didn't have an alarm on its back window. The rusted bars were the only security feature she'd seen. Plus, the three men who'd been in there earlier that evening.

She used her sweater to clear any particularly sharp pieces jutting out from the windowsill; then, teeth clenched, she slipped her slim form through the gap created by the smashed glass and broken bar.

It took some finagling. Her shoulder scraped glass protruding like teeth. She winced, exhaling as she tried to avoid drawing blood, and then, after a shimmy of the hips, her legs scraping against the other metal bar, she slipped into the police station, dropping to the ground with a quiet *thump*.

Cora held her breath, listening intently. She crouched on her heels and then began to move slowly towards the door. She frowned as she moved; by the looks of things, she had found a break room with a vending machine, a desk, and some well-worn furniture.

She continued forward, approached a wooden door, eased it open, and stepped out into a dark hall. Down to the right, she spotted a set of holding cells. Empty, the metal doors left open, keys on a hook on the wall.

She kept moving, heading away from the cells, and she spotted an open, opaque, glass door. She recognized it as the door leading to the lobby. This was where she had heard the voice of the captain yelling at someone.

It took her a few moments, but then, she spotted an office.

On the sheer opposite side of the building from the cell doors, nestled against the back and guarded by a thick, oak door, with a nameplate that had faded.

"Bingo," she murmured to herself.

On the balls of her feet, she began to approach.

She reached the door, and it was locked.

She frowned, glancing along the walls in the hope of anymore keys on hooks. But she wasn't so lucky. And so, instead, she tried the door handle. Locked. She moved along, looking for a separate entrance. But there was none. Her eyes found a vent, and she wondered if she ought to try to push it in and climb through.

But then, she shot a look at her phone. It was late. Very late. The longer she was here, the more chance there was that something would go wrong. That was another tactical rule. In and out, fast.

As she considered this, she felt a flicker of fear; memories returning. Dark, crushing memories.

In and out. And she *hadn't* been fast. She could remember that horrible event, years ago. They had captured her; she had stayed too long, looking for one of her platoon members.

But he had been captured already. She hadn't known it at the time.

She could remember their threats. Remember their hands against her skin, forcing her forward, rough movements, guns against her neck.

As the enemy had pushed her ahead of them, guiding her into a labyrinth, the scent of the place had left her nauseous. But the knowledge of what was to come—the torture, the psychological abuse—had left her nearly catatonic. It was all well and good to act tough. But until one was truly tested, the act was just that. Pretend.

And she had learned the hard way that pain could get anyone to talk.

Images and horrible memories played. Her shoulder and arm throbbed. She felt a sudden urge, a longing. She wanted to find a drink. Wanted to pop some pills.

She held her breath, counting slowly in her mind. When she opened her eyes again, a surge of fear flooded through her. She didn't like locked doors. She had spent weeks behind a particularly heinous set of barriers.

She took a step back, and her foot lashed out. It collided with the door. She stepped back and tried again. Once, twice. At last, the lock shattered. The door groaned and slowly opened.

She breathed heavily, staring into the office. A few splinters of shattered wood around the doorjamb angled towards the floor. One large splinter twisted and swayed, stuck by a single strand of wood, and then fell, hitting the ground. She stepped over it, entering the office.

She could still feel the memories playing, could feel the slow chill along her arms.

She swallowed and forced her mind to refocus. It wasn't the same as dealing with her emotions, speaking about them, finding someone to be vulnerable with; she hadn't wept about these moments. But what she managed was to suppress it. To bury it, like pushing a bottle full of air under dark water.

It took effort, exertion, holding the bottle there, as it attempted to rise to the surface again.

But it was better to keep it hidden than to allow the darkness complete control.

That's how people ended up like Adelaide.

And now, Cora was moving, quickly. There was a computer. She didn't bother with this. She didn't have the time figure out a password.

Against the wall, she spotted a metal file cabinet; it took her a few moments, but she found the keys next to the Sheriff's desk.

She tried the keys.

"Shit." They didn't go to the cabinet. She tried the keys to the drawer beneath the computer desk.

It opened. The drawer was empty.

She frowned, tossing the keys back onto the desk and approaching the file cabinet, her eyes flashing.

If she had to treat this like she had the door, she wouldn't hesitate. There was a time that Cora might simply have shot the locks. But of course, she had left her gun back home. Eventually, she would have to relinquish it; for now, though, she still did have a utility knife that she kept with her at all times.

For a SEAL, it was essentially the same as a keychain ring.

She pulled the utility knife from her belt and approached the file cabinet. It didn't look like a particularly secure cabinet. And so, she began to pry and finagle. A few flecks of greenish paint fluttered where she worked.

She winced. She didn't want to leave too much evidence of what she'd been up to. Then again, if that was the case, she probably shouldn't have shattered the window.

Cora continued to finagle with her knife in the lock.

In the end, though when the thing didn't open, she changed tactics. Instead of trying to slip a bolt, she simply tried to bend the metal, giving her fingers purchase.

She managed, using her knife, to create a bit of space between the file cabinet's drawer and the frame.

Then, this done, glancing around, she found one of the splinters of wood from the door, grabbed it, jammed it into the gap she had created, and then went to work with her knife, to create an even wider gap.

It took a few minutes, her fingers aching by the end. But then, with a satisfying *click*, she managed to push the metal twist lock out of the way.

The piece of wood fell into the drawer, no longer secured by pressure. And she slowly opened the drawer.

She stared inside, her heart pounding.

The manila folders were arranged alphabetically; it took her a moment, but she read through various items. Her heart fell; these weren't case files. Rather, it looked to have something to do with taxes. Another was a ledger, containing numbers that didn't make sense to her.

One of the folders, though, she noticed, was left unmarked. So naturally, this was the one she placed on the desk, opening the folder, scanning more numbers. By the looks of things, it was payments. Deposits into the police department's main account.

She wasn't an accountant, so most of this was guesswork, but she did notice something. Some of the payments had fees associated with them. Her finger trailed along, following the column of information. The one that caught her attention most was marked, *international processing.*

The four lump sum payments, each totaling at least $50,000, caught her attention.

She whistled softly. Why was a small Police Department in Westville receiving $50,000 deposits from some international source? She tried to make more sense of the numbers she'd found but without context, much of it didn't make sense.

As she considered this, though, she froze.

She had heard a sound.

She turned slowly, prickles along her spine.

There were voices coming from inside the building; they weren't drawing nearer, but they were getting louder

An icy prickle of fear shot up her spine. With rapid, lightning-fast motions, she slipped the folder back into the file cabinet, closed the drawer, kicked some of the splintered wood out of the way, hastened to the door, glanced into the hall, made sure the coast was clear, then slipped into the hall, shutting the door with her elbow.

And now she could make out the content of the voices.

The loudest one, which she recognized from the last time she'd come, was shouting, "We had a deal; if you go back on that deal, you're going to regret it!"

There was some dark muttering. And then a much quieter, calmer response. The second voice she couldn't make out, but she knew she didn't recognize it.

She caught a couple of words, and they sounded heavily accented.

Not one of the other officers she had met then.

"I'm serious," the first voice snapped, "if you're not careful, you're heading for a heap of trouble."

Cora was caught in indecision. On one hand, she wanted to get out of there as fast as she could but on the other, this sounded important; why had they come back to the office? She had seen them leave... something had changed.

Who was the captain of police meeting with?

That soft, velvety, calm voice was replying once more. And, reaching a decision, as she took careful steps down the hall, towards the direction of the open door that led into the main area, she could make out this second man's words. "Please calm down," he was saying. "We both know you don't want to be yelling at me."

There was something cold about the tone. Something frigid. The calm, the quiet wasn't that of a subordinate in fear. Rather, it was the voice of a man who knew he was in control.

Cora heard another voice join the conversation. She recognized it as Hurley's, the red headed ogler from before.

"Mister, you wouldn't want to back out of a deal with us, would you? That could be dangerous for your health."

Cora listened, her skin prickling. A third voice joined. This one, the handsome police officer. "Shut up, Hurley. What we mean to say is, we had a business arrangement. We thought it was mutually beneficial..."

Cora moved closer to the door. Forms moved against a backdrop of glowing, yellow light.

Why had they returned?

By the sound of things, at least, they didn't know she was there.

But it was only a matter of time.

She glanced over her shoulder towards the break room she had entered through. If she was smart, now would be the time to make her getaway.

As she leaned against the door, her phone suddenly began to vibrate.

She tensed, glancing down, grateful that she had left the ringer off this time.

She reached into her pocket, turning the phone off, just in case, and then returning her attention to the voices on the other side of the door.

"We all want this to work; it's been mutually beneficial, and we've done our part, and kept our noses clean. And you've been able to do what you need to do for your clients," the handsome policeman was saying. "Now why don't we all just calm down; we can all benefit from this. There's no point in making things more difficult than they need to be, am I right?"

Cora moved, placing her eyes to the keyhole; she spotted the redhaired figure nearest the door. She shifted, moving her gaze, and then she spotted a man in a black, expensive suit. A gold chain rested on his collar.

The man was smaller than the others. And yet, as he adjusted his sleeves, he seemed perfectly at ease. He said, in that same velvety, smooth, calm voice, "The fee has changed. We haven't had as much success here as we would have liked. And from what the young one tells me, there are people still asking about the merchandise. Why is that?"

There was a sudden silence. Cora frowned, trying to make sense of this.

But then, the voice of the captain interjected, "Now hang on, I'm sure that's not what Hurley meant, is it Hurley?"

"No, of course not. No. I just meant that we should be careful in case anyone *does* come around asking about those girls."

"The merchandise," said the man with the gold chain, his voice firm. Through the keyhole, Cora couldn't make out the man's face, as he was standing too far back.

Now, though, her mind was spinning. Clearly, the police officers were corrupt. The captain himself was in on it.

And the voice of the man with the golden chain was giving her the sense that he was clearly involved in the disappearance of at least Caitlin, if not the other women. *Merchandise.* She scowled and then she heard the sound of footsteps.

"Look, I have a gift for you in my office. I feel like we may have gotten off on the wrong foot. Let me grab it. I'm sure we'll figure this out."

As the footsteps approached, Cora's eyes widened; she turned sharply, moving fast. She hastened to the room with the open window and slipped inside, shutting the door just as she heard the rattle of the handle from the opaque door.

The footsteps were now coming up the hall; the voices continued, calmer now, controlled.

As Cora hastened to the open window, careful to avoid the shattered glass, she went still.

More voices. This time coming from the direction of the alley. And these voices were unfamiliar, but they shared the same accent as the man with the golden chain.

She paused; peering out, two men were standing in the mouth of the alley, their hands hooked in their belts. One of them had a gun jammed in the back of his waistband. The other a gun in his hand, examining it. They both spoke nonchalantly, facing a large, black truck that had been parked half on the curb.

Cora cursed. If she went out the window, they'd see her. If she stayed here, though, it was only a matter of time until they found her.

She listened to the voices out in the alley and then returned her attention once again, to the voices behind her, coming from the hallway.

"I must have left it in the break room," the voice was saying.

She tensed. She heard movement, rapid footsteps. And then, the door handle to the break room began to turn.

She glanced rapidly around, panicked. Window wasn't an option. They were going to find the glass. Going to find the broken bar.

The police here were crooked, though. They were clearly on the take.

And if they found her, and realized she'd been listening, there was no telling what they would do. Had they killed those three young women?

But Cora didn't have time to speculate. She hastened forward, low, and moved behind an alcove created by a sink, and a protruding vending machine.

Her shoulder pressed against the vending machine, and she felt the warmth of the metal. The thing was vibrating silently and then, the door to the break room opened.

She watched, scarcely daring to breathe as a figure with an impressive, neatly trimmed beard, and stoic posture emerged.

The tall man glanced side to side, frowning.

And then he went still. He was staring at the glass shattered beneath the broken window. He took a step into the room.

"Boys, come here!" he said, his voice urgent. "Come here, right

65

now!"

She heard more footsteps, and couldn't risk trying to peak now, and so she pressed back, hidden against the large vending machine. She waited, quiet, heart pounding fast.

CHAPTER NINE

The vehicle jolted to a halt, and Caitlin seized her opportunity. She grabbed at the hand of the girl at her side, whispering fiercely, "Now!"

She'd risked a few more peeks from beneath her blindfold, but they'd been going too fast up until this point. The young woman at her side lay as if dead, though, refusing to rise.

Caitlin's heart jolted. "Come on!" she whispered. "Now or never!"

But the girl was crying again, shaking her head.

Caitlin faced a horrible decision. She'd already stayed behind once before for the girl. And now, in the distance, she spotted where they were being taken. The walls were topped with barbed wire. It looked like a maximum-security prison from where she stood. There was no hope of breeching it.

No, no she couldn't stay. If they took her within, there would be no coming back out.

And so, with a final, futile tug at the arm of the woman by her side, Caitlin abandoned this course and instead bolted over the side of the jeep, haring into the jungle.

No time for subtlety.

Only fleet-footed action.

Her hands were still free, her blindfold now discarded. And so, she sprinted, her legs wobbly, but her feet determined as she stumbled forward. She hit one knee after a few steps, but surged back up a moment later, careening onward.

Voices shouted behind her. She heard the sound of a gunshot. The tree off to her left exploded. Twigs and leaves tumbled from shuddering boughs.

The voices shouted. Footsteps came in hot pursuit.

Another gunshot, and this time she couldn't trace the bullet impact, but at the same time, she heard a voice yell in fury. The gunshots stopped.

They wanted her alive.

This frightened her even more than the thought of death.

And so, she tore relentlessly through the jungle.

But it wasn't like the movies. It wasn't as if she had open space between occasional trees over which to sprint through the dark. Rather, it was more like a maze. Ducking a tangle of branches draped with moss. Squeezing through a tight gap created by boulders jutting up like stone teeth. She scraped under another bow and cursed as something slithered beneath her outstretched hand. Insects were already nipping at her. Golden eyes watched her from where they were perched in a tree above.

But she kept going.

The sound of pursuit continued from behind.

She slipped into a boggy area, her foot drenched. They'd taken her shoes and socks, most likely to prevent this very thing. Her toes were cold now, slippery as she pushed out onto easier terrain.

The oppressive dark, the tweet, shiver, and whisper of the jungle all whispered threats in her ears.

She wasn't going to make it.

She couldn't do this.

But she pushed the accusing voices aside and continued her breakneck pace through the dark, hastening ever forward.

As she moved, her heart thundered. As her feet struck the muddy ground, she felt a rising sense of fear.

Shouts now. Branches breaking.

The pursuers behind her came en masse.

She couldn't count them. But bright lights shone from flashlights, spotlighting her trail. Seeking her in the dark.

For every attempt at finding a path she managed, they had multiple attempts, given their number.

Plus, they were likely more familiar with this foreign terrain.

She could hear the sound of them drawing nearer.

Ahead, to the right, she spotted a flash of light. Someone was already next to her, overpassed her. Ahead of her. Their light continued forward, as if they thought she were still out in front.

And so, she reached a horrible decision.

She dropped to the ground, wincing as she did. Breathing far, far too loudly for her comfort.

Her mind was racing, her body tense. Sweat slicked her and mingled with the dirt to create a sort of paste that latched onto her skin.

She bit her lip, tasting salt, and cowering beneath long leaves of ground cover that extended and twirled above her.

Exhausted, sleep and food deprived, thirsty, and with bleeding feet, she stayed put. Prone in some bush in some God-forsaken jungle, listening to these monsters creep after her.

Their heavy breathing and whispered comments reached her ears, sending probing shivers along her spine.

She waited, poised.

They were bound to pass, weren't they?

They had to be passing by now.

She thought she heard movement behind her, but then sudden silence.

And for a moment, the jungle returned to its nocturnal stirrings.

She shifted restlessly, wincing against an itch in her spine. Against something brushing her toes. Every touch, every motion filling her mind with thoughts of poisonous spiders, venomous snakes, and long-toothed jaguars.

The fear alone was nearly crippling.

Cautiously, heart pounding, she began to move slowly, slipping from under the brush. Her hands pressed to soft ground, creasing mud, and she pushed slowly up, peering side to side.

No sign of anyone behind her.

She began to turn slowly.

Click.

A light beamed down on her.

She froze. Her tongue trapped against the roof of her mouth.

The man with the light said something harsh, raised his gun and pointed it at her. She stared down the barrel, frozen in place.

They wanted her alive.

There were worse things than death.

And so, she spun on her heel, sprinting the other way.

But she only made it two paces.

Two more men had emerged from the trees behind her. Their hands shot out, catching her, and holding her fast.

She yelled in horror, kicking and slapping, trying to break free.

But the men were hitting her now, yelling. The one behind her was chuckling as he approached, holstering his gun, keeping his light fixated on her struggling form.

CHAPTER TEN

Cora hid behind the vending machine, her one hand pressed against the warm plating on the back. Her shoulder vibrating softly with the motion of the appliance. She no longer peeked out into the office, preferring to stay back, hiding in the dark.

Voices filled the office now. Light bloomed.

"See that?" came the captain's voice. "Glass—someone broke in. Shit! Think it was..."

"Nah—no," said the older brother's voice. He dropped his tone to a whisper. "Why do that and come here anyway? No—no, not him."

Then, Hurley whispered, "What about that bitch from earlier?"

A moment of silence.

The older brother whispered back, "You might be right. Dad, we had this girl come in here. Tatted up, said she was military. Friend of Addie. She was looking around. Asking about Caitlin."

Another pause. Longer this time than the first one.

And then a harsh breath of air. "Shit...What was her name?"

"Cora...something. Shins?"

"No, Hurley, it wasn't *Shins.*"

"Alright, genius, you tell me then. What was it?"

Another pause.

"Are you idiots telling me you didn't get her name?"

"It was late. She was feisty, Dad. Don't worry. I'm sure it's nothing. It's not like she could find anything."

The shadows were moving again. Only three of them. The man with the golden chain and expensive suit had been left back in the lobby by the look and sounds of things.

Good thing too...She didn't see a way out of this without hurting folk.

And already, three against one, wasn't going to be pretty.

"Man...you don't think she was one of the girls, was she?" said the captain, his voice quiet.

A dark chuckle from Hurley. "Ghost of some hot slut come back to haunt us, huh?"

The others chuckled as well.

Cora's eyes narrowed. She reached out slowly, unplugging the vending machine. The vibrating suddenly ceased. The machine went quiet. She then used her knife to cut through the wire at the base of the machine. Then, she hefted the wire in one hand, the knife in the other.

"Hey..." Hurley said suddenly. "Look—did...did you see th—"

He didn't have time to finish. Cora had been waiting until one of the shadows came near, behind the desk, closest to the vending machine.

It just so happened to be the redhead. He stepped towards her, investigating the suddenly unilluminated machine. But as he drew close, Cora burst forward with a shout.

The thing about fighting in the military...

The point wasn't to make it last long.

It wasn't a sport.

It was a tool meant to contain a physical threat in as short amount a time as possible with as little damage taken as possible.

The damage dispensed to the threat?

Dealer's choice mostly.

And so, she darted forward, fast. She used the cable she'd taken from behind the vending machine to wrap the thick wire around Hurley's neck. He squawked like a chicken, his Adam's apple bobbing past her knuckles.

But he didn't have time to speak on account of the makeshift black noose tight around his throat.

As he tried to reach her, to stop her, she slashed his knuckles with her knife.

The yelp turned into a gargle. She twisted, squeezing hard, using the tension of both wrists to yank back on the wire.

The other men were shouting. The older brother was pulling his weapon, aiming at her, trying to sight past his gurgling brother.

Cora pivoted.

She shoved Hurley into his brother and the bullet went wide as the gunshot was redirected at the very last moment.

She was already moving, though, scrambling across the desk and lunging for the captain.

The man with the stately goatee and thick brow yelled. He stumbled back, pulling desperately at his own weapon which had caught in his holster.

"Small-town punks!" she yelled. And then she tackled the cop around the waist, brought him hard to the ground. She pulled his gun

71

for him, unhooking it from where it had snared on a brass button of a leather-seemed holster. More about showcase than practicality.

She turned with her gun, laying flat on the captain's chest, and using him as a pivot point.

Again, Hurley was in the way.

But he wasn't *her* brother.

She fired twice.

Hit the older brother in the knee.

He yelled, dropping suddenly. His gun hit the ground.

Hurley was going for his own weapon now, having regained some of his breath. But she hit him in the hand, sending him spinning. He yelped as he stumbled into the wall.

"My hand!" he screamed, blood flowing freely.

"I was aiming for your head," she muttered.

She'd gotten a bit rusty on aiming from a prone position.

It just so happened the position was also the chest of a wheezing police captain.

Cora heard the sound of shouting. Of slamming doors. The whir of wheels, suggesting the truck she'd seen earlier was beating a hasty, tactical retreat.

Cora disentangled herself from the police captain, rising to her feet slowly. When the man reached out, attempting to snare her foot, she kicked his wrist, receiving a grunt of pain in return.

She stepped on his arm, and snapped, "Stay down."

Gun in hand, corralling the other two officers who were clutching their hand and leg respectively, she sidestepped towards the door, breathing in and out.

She watched the officers writhe, feeling sweat down her spine. She kept her voice tense as she murmured. "I know what's going on here. I heard *everything*." She added a lie. "I've taken photos of your financial files, and audio recordings of your conversations. If *anything* happens to Jamie Johnson, or her family—if she gets so much as a parking ticket, I'll release it all to the FBI." Then, she reached the door, shoulders pressed against the wood.

The scent of blood lingered in the air. The faint mewls of pain brought back other memories which she attempted to suppress. She cleared her throat, forcing her mind to refocus. "And," she added, "if any of you come after me..." She pointed her gun at each of them individually, raising an eyebrow as she did. "Are we clear?"

The captain snarled at her, sitting up now, rubbing his chest, his face red.

She repeated. "Are we clear?"

He spat to the side.

She paused for a moment, then shrugged. "Fine then."

She raised her gun, aiming at his head.

"Wait—wait! No!" The captain yelled, hands out suddenly. His perfect little goatee trembled on the edge of his chin. "W-we're clear!" he stammered. "Crystal clear. No one is going to come after you. Jamie is fine. We...we're not bad men. We just..." he swallowed. "Just looked the other way a couple of times. It wasn't like the girls were safe anyway. It wasn't like."

Cora glared. "Where are they? Where is Caitlin? The others too? Erin, Cynthia?"

"Shut up, Dad," snapped one of the brothers. Through the pain, lips clenched, she couldn't determine which one had spoken.

But their old man snarled. "You shut up. This was your damn idea, now sit there and bleed, you imbecile."

Cora tapped her foot impatiently, regaining their attention. "Tell me," she said firmly, "what did you do to the girls?" Her gun began to raise again.

"Nothing—nothing!" the captain shouted. "We just...we didn't...we let some things slide. We don't even know who they took. We just...we just were paid to be quiet. To look the other way. We don't know who they are. Don't know anything about it. P-please!" he sobbed. "Don't shoot me."

Cora was seriously considering it. But then she sighed, lowered her gun again and began to move.

As she fled into the hall, she broke into a sprint, determined not to give the men a chance to come after her.

She checked her phone.

It had recorded everything.

First thing, she'd send it all to Saul at the FBI. Her partner would know what to do with it. For now, her threat would have to keep Jamie safe, but Cora was also going to let the Johnsons know it would be good to make themselves scarce for a couple of weeks.

She sprinted through the glass door, into the lobby. Pausing long enough only to make sure the coast was clear.

But there was no sign of the man with the golden chain and swanky suit.

She moved hastily out the front doors.

No sign of the truck either. Only a shade of rubber over the lip of the concrete curb.

She heard sirens now, in the distance.

Police? Ambulance?

She didn't want to stick around to find out.

She broke into a sprint, racing towards her van.

She believed the captain when he was begging with her. He didn't know who he'd been turning a blind eye for. And even if he did, she hadn't had the time to extract the information. But judging by his blubbering, his sudden desperation at the thought of being shot, she was confident he would have turned over anything to spare his skin if he could have.

But she didn't need him as her guiding light.

Rather, the compass she was relying on, her own eyes, suggested the man she was after had just fled in that truck. The golden chain, the suit, the velvety voice had been that of a man in charge.

She hastened towards the minivan she'd borrowed. The car wasn't going to break any speed records. But right now, all she needed was to catch up with the bossman.

She felt a pulse of exhilaration as she slipped into the van, gunned the engine, and peeled away from the curb. She raced down the street, in the direction the truck had been angled.

It wasn't like Westville had many roads leading in or out.

Only two, in fact.

Which meant she had a coin flip of a chance to find them. She would have to push the van to its limit.

But the benefit she had was she knew that most of the Westville police force was still bleeding out back in their office. The attention would, undoubtedly, divert to them.

Whereas the man with the chain would want to keep on the down low. He'd likely observe the speed-limits, unaware that most of the cops who'd normally monitor that sort of thing were currently en route back to their station.

Speeding.

Not exactly the *best* advantage to have in a rust bucket like this.

But the only chance she had.

A coin flip she chose the right road out of town.

Another coin flip that she'd be able to go fast enough without being pulled over to find the bastard.

But one way or another, she felt that same surge of lacing

adrenaline.

She couldn't help but drum her hands against the steering wheel, letting loose a sudden scream of exhilaration.

And this time, it had nothing to do with damn pills.

As she sped forward, she paused long enough to lift her phone. She needed to warn Jamie. Needed to text Saul.

As her phone lifted, though, she frowned at the call she'd missed.

Commander Grayson.

She let out a huff of air. Why was he calling her? Just checking in?

No time to muse on it, though.

She raced through the small-town streets, blowing a stop sign, angry red taillights glaring at the rough asphalt.

As she called Jamie, she kept her head on a swivel, glancing side to side, looking for any sign of the truck. Only one hotel in the area, though. No, she doubted the man with the golden chain was going to stay local.

Especially not after the ruckus back at the station.

No, men like that—Men who exuded control—they retreated to places where they *had* control.

Fifty-fifty, she'd chosen the right road.

CHAPTER ELEVEN

She'd passed two police cars as she sped twenty miles over the speed limit, racing down the highway. Both had been heading in the opposite direction, speeding towards the police station.

One had even slowed, beginning to wobble as if wanting to turn and go after her, but then had thought better of it and continued down the highway in the opposite direction.

She watched the flashing red and blue lights in her rearview mirror, feeling a slow surge of relief.

Jamie was warned. Doors were locked and windows were closed. Her mother was going to take the weekend off from Sunday school. On top of it, she'd also sent the audio recording to Agent Brady. She hadn't had time to fill him in on any of the details, but those could wait.

Now, her attention had been captured by a vehicle in a gas station off the side of the road.

The *reason* it had caught her attention, was the way it had veered across three lanes the moment the sirens had started and the flashing lights had appeared on the opposite road.

Plus, the vehicle was a large, dark truck.

She tried to move surreptitiously, slowing now as she approached the gas station. Her window was open, allowing a wind current to flutter through the vehicle, ruffling her shoulder-length hair.

She reached the gas station, moving slowly, pulling up to a pump on the exact opposite side of the station.

She watched two men emerge from the dark truck, glancing around. One of them looked straight at her, and she pretended as if she was checking her phone for something.

When she looked up again, the front door to the truck had opened.

A man was sitting there, straight-backed, hands folded neatly. She glimpsed a flash of gold around his neck.

A jolt of exhilaration.

She'd found them.

This was it.

She swallowed, tense, staring towards the truck as the men

pretended to be fueling it, but mostly just watched the disappearing cop car, waiting and muttering to each other.

Another one of the men glanced towards her.

She winced, looking out the window now, studying the front of the mini gas station store.

But when she looked over, the two men who'd been guarding the alley earlier were staring straight at her.

She let out a puff of air.

A choice, she had a choice.

A direct confrontation?

All three of those men were armed. And this time, she didn't have the advantage of surprise.

On the other hand, if she let them get away, she wasn't sure she'd have another chance to find them. The license plate, she felt certain, was fake or stolen.

She gave a little wave towards the men staring at her. One of them scowled and began moving towards her. His hand snuck inside his jacket.

The man inside the truck adjusted a briefcase at his feet.

His socks were black, his shoes polished, but red leather. His briefcase was similarly expensive, with a small, golden snake etched on the side.

Cora pressed her teeth together.

One of the men had postured by a pump fifteen feet away. He wasn't coming any closer, but he was pulling something from his jacket.

She reached a decision.

They weren't cops. They weren't going to stop her, speak with her.

Whatever they were, their body language was clear.

They intended to shoot her dead for no other reason than *just in case.*

And so, she floored the pedal, cursing and ducking. Bullets flew after her. The back windshield shattered, but she kept going, speeding as she hastened back onto the street, leaving rubber against the ground and spinning off to a small parking lot. She drove over concrete barriers into an adjoining lot outside a closed fast-food place. The bullets stopped. The truck's brights glared at her and the vehicle pulled back onto the highway, speeding rapidly away from her.

She watched it merge, breathing heavily. She tried to turn, but the car wasn't moving.

She cursed, trying again. But having glided to a halt, bumping against the front of a store window, her vehicle was no longer working.

A stray bullet? Had she hit something, bumping over the concrete barrier?

"Shit!" she screamed, slamming a hand against the steering wheel. The adrenaline continued to bruit through her veins, and she closed her eyes against a sudden jolt of a piercing headache.

She glared into the rearview mirror, twisting to watch the final glimpse of red brake lights as the truck disappeared up the road, sweeping under a bridge.

She exhaled slowly, forcing her mind to focus.

Emotions were only useful insofar as they aided in the mission.

And now, the next step was clear.

She pulled her phone, her hand shaking somewhat, the adrenaline rapidly cycling even still. She lifted the phone, waiting for it to connect. And then, once again in control of her emotions, she said, quietly, "Jamie—listen to me. Change of plans. I'm going to need you to report your mother's vehicle stolen. Right now. If at all possible, go across the street and ask to borrow a neighbor's phone to make a call. That way, you'll have an alibi when the cops come calling. Yes—yes, you'll need one. It will be fine. Just do what I say."

Cora listened to the reply, but she was only half paying attention, as her heart continued to beat a drum.

She then pushed out of the wreckage of the van and broke into a jog, phone still glued to her cheek as she hastened away from the sputtering van.

That taken care of, other thoughts cycled through her mind.

She pictured the truck, the man in the front seat. The golden chain...and...the snake emblem on his briefcase.

She frowned as she considered this last part. Then, she said into the phone, "Sorry, I have to go. Please—do what I say." And then she hung up, breaking into a sprint now, racing away from the parking lot, from the van.

The police would still be scrambling in the small town. But eventually, even startled hounds caught a scent.

She needed another course of action.

One thing was certain, Caitlin Johnson *hadn't* run away. She'd been taken. Along with the other girls from Westville, no doubt. And possibly many others.

CHAPTER TWELVE

Cora slowed to a jog, then to a rapid walk as she reached an underpass, stepping along a sidewalk in the dark. Behind her, a constant wail in the night, she heard the blare of sirens.

Her mind, however, was captured by something else entirely.

The emblem on the briefcase.

Possibly a company emblem? Maybe a designer bag?

It was the only thing she could think of.

The license plate number was also seared into her mind. Worth a shot—though this, she guessed, wouldn't be fruitful.

Men with guns who bribed cops weren't generally the sort to give away their identities via the DMV. She moved hastily along the underpass, head ducked, hands in her pockets, moving hurriedly. She needed a way to trace that snake logo.

Needed someone who could access the information in particular databases that she no longer had access to.

She sighed as she considered it, then pulled her phone from her pocket. She hesitated a moment, considering her options.

Commander Grayson came to mind...

But no, the commander played things by the book. Same as her old partner, Saul.

But what about...

She bit her lip, pausing for a moment in the underpass. Then nodding to herself as she reached a decision.

Yes, *he* might be willing to help.

She dialed the number from memory. Phone numbers, like license plates, were easy for her to memorize.

She waited a few moments, willing the phone to connect despite the late hour.

But it didn't.

She frowned, considered, then tried again.

Once more, she waited patiently, listening to the dial tone. And only after the fifth ring, did someone answer.

"H-hello?" came a croaking voice. "Who's there?"

Cora's eyes widened and she felt her heart skip at the familiar voice. How long had it been? Five years? Six?

She said quickly, "This is Cora Shields. Hey Sam—how are you?"

A sudden pause. Then a quick inhale. "Holy shit. How's it going Cobra?"

She winced at the old nickname. Then again, the snake tattoo on her right arm had been inked specifically because of the moniker. "It's going," she said hurriedly. "Hey, Sam, I wish I could catch up, but this is kinda—"

"Damn, this about the funeral? Man, Cobra, I was gonna. Really gonna. Just things got away from me. You know. Work n' all. I know you were close with Adder."

Cobra and Adder. Cora sighed. Another life, another time. Standing there in the underpass, sweating profusely, breathing heavy, it all seemed like a mirage. Silly almost.

But there had been nothing silly about the men who'd given her that name.

Nothing silly about the apologetic, spurting way that Sam spoke. She'd singlehandedly seen the Navy medic rescue six men out from under mortar fire while running on a broken leg with absolutely no regard for his own safety.

In fact, that was why he'd been discharged. His act of heroism had seen him too injured to continue in the service. More shrapnel in his leg than bone now, according to the last she'd heard.

"Sam, I'm not calling about the funeral," she cut in urgently. "I'm looking for a favor."

Another pause. "What type of favor?" A note of suspicion had now crept into his voice.

She shifted uncomfortably. "I'm...I'm looking to track someone. He's got a—"

"Hello no, Cora," Sam said suddenly. And she knew he was serious as he'd used her actual name. "I'm not in that game anymore. I whittle."

"Excuse me?"

"You heard me. I whittle. Try Johnny. He's in South America somewhere. I'm sure he'd love to hear from you."

"Very funny."

"No, shit. I mean it. Johnny...he's different now."

Cora frowned. "Look, Sam, it's important. Addie had a daughter. She's been taken—"

"Hey—hey don't tell me that shit! Stop. It's depressing. I can't help

80

you, Cora. Like literally can't. I don't have access anymore. I really do whittle. I own my own woodshop. Call Johnny—look. I gotta go. Sorry about missing the funeral."

"Sam! Wait."

"No, gotta go. Seeya!"

He hung up, and Cora held back a shout of frustration. She stared in fury at the phone, glaring. She paused for a moment, considering her options.

Johnny?

That Italian prick had caused her more grief than the rest of them combined. Then again, that was somewhat par for the course when SEALs decided to flout regulation and start seeing each other.

And Johnny had definitely seen Cora. And then, after things had ended in—quite literally—a fiery fashion, Cora and Johnny had sworn they'd never see each other again.

She shifted from side to side, trying to think of another option.

Maybe she ought to just risk Agent Brady, Saul *had* said she should call when she needed.

She nibbled on her lip, considering the options.

But then she sighed, shaking her head.

She knew what Saul would say.

Besides, the old man's bedtime was nine p.m. sharp. He wouldn't answer anyhow.

"Shit," she muttered, raising her phone again.

Did she remember Johnny's number? So much of that man she'd tried to force *out* of her memory. But as she considered it, the numbers came back to her, floating to the surface like more bed memories.

Reluctantly, and with an air of petulance, she jammed the digits into her phone. Her thumb hovered over the green phone icon. She waited a moment, and then, with an act of will, she pressed dial.

As the phone started to connect, she glanced down the underpass, watching as a car moved towards her, headlights bright. They had their high beams on. She tensed, her shadow cast behind her like a long streak of ink. She held out a hand, blocking the glare from the lights.

The car was moving slowly...too slowly, wasn't it?

She began to move now, turning and striding rapidly up the underpass. She waited, listening to the approaching car, ears attentive. She lifted her phone in front of her, using the reflection to watch the motion of the oncoming vehicle.

It didn't stop though. Didn't slow.

Just kept moving, at the same snail's pace, past her, then out the other side of the underpass.

She breathed a sigh of relief...

But relief was short lived as she heard the voice.

"Hey? Cora? That you?"

She stared at the phone where she held it away from herself as if attempting to keep it at arm's length. For a moment, she considered dropping the thing and beating a tactical retreat.

But she needed the help, needed the information.

For now, she was flying blind.

Caitlin was still out there. The daughter she'd never known her friend had.

Adder and Cobra.

Never again. Addie dead by her own hand.

Cora felt a shiver of horror at the thought, shaking her head in frustration. Then, like swallowing something nasty, or ripping a band-aid, in one rapid motion, she placed the phone back to her cheek. Somehow, the cold of the device made her skin crawl.

"John," she said simply. He'd always hated when people called him John. Said it made him think of his mother. And so, she repeated it, "John."

"Cora," he replied, curt, tense.

It had been three years since they'd last seen each other. And...he sounded exactly the same. Two parts smug, six parts arrogant and ten parts asshole.

"I called Sam first," Cora said quickly, feeling as if this were an important piece of information to share. "But he couldn't help."

Johnny said, "So you need my help? What with?"

She scowled at this interpretation. It was true...she just didn't like hearing him say it. She sighed, picturing her old flame's rugged features. He'd been built like a gymnast. Average height with deceptively strong muscles on a trim frame. One of his eyes had a scar along the lid, up to the hairline—testament to a close encounter with a knife-wielding terrorist. His arms were similarly scarred, and his hair was always cut short. A neat, military cut for a man who otherwise made a habit of flouting the rules.

This, of course, was why Sam had recommended Johnny to begin with.

If ever there was someone she could work with outside the usual bounds of acceptable conduct, it was her ex.

But she hadn't anticipated exactly how much talking with him would *grate* on her.

She paused, inhaling sharply through her teeth. She emerged from the underpass now, out into the moonlit sky again, towards a row of security lights lining a metal barrier protecting a switchback and a sharp drop.

As she moved, she said, "I need you to run a plate. You still able to do that?"

"Able to? What do you mean able to?"

"Nothing. Just asking if you can do that."

"What's in it for me?"

"Christ, Johnny," she snapped. "You think I wanted to make this call?"

"Nah, definitely not. You haven't called in three years. I shoulda figured the one time you pick up the damn thing, you only do it 'cus you need something."

Her temper flared. "Hold on one moment!" she snapped. "That's not fair!"

"Which part?"

She considered this. Then huffed in frustration. In a way, she supposed he did have a point. She hadn't made a habit of calling any of her old SEAL buddies. She'd wanted a clean break. Especially after how all of it had ended.

Now...

With Addie...

With Johnny...

She was feeling the slow prickle of regret. And no small amount of guilt.

Which, of course, just made her angrier.

"You know what, forget it!" she snapped. "I'll figure it out myself."

She hung up, marching up the sidewalk, beneath the streetlights. The bright glare of the white bulbs cast her shadow in constant motion, first before her then behind as she moved up the road. No sound of sirens now. No passing cars.

In the distance, along the highway, she spotted the occasional beacon of headlights, but otherwise she felt very much alone.

Her phone began to ring.

She scowled at it.

It continued ringing, somehow feeling more insistent than normal. Perhaps that was just because of the source of the call.

She answered, "What?"

"No," Johnny snapped.

"What?"

"No. We're not doing this. You don't get to beg for help, hang up, act like a spoiled teenage brat then expect me to *beg you* to *help you*."

He sounded like he was just getting started. So, she hung up again.

This time he didn't call back.

She stared at her phone, feeling that same sense of guilt. She sighed, rubbing a hand across her face. Then, muttering darkly to herself, she placed a call again.

"Feel better?" Johnny said when he answered.

"Not really. You know...this is why I didn't call. I don't have time to deal with the attitude, John."

"Alright, Cobra," he retorted, fully knowing just how much she loathed the nickname.

For a moment, they both remained on the line, both breathing heavily, both clearly irritated. But then, Cora, biting back whatever retort she could feel burbling in her throat, said, "Can you run a plate or not, Johnny?"

"Already got the database up, Cora. Just wanted you to ask nice is all."

Cora, still frowning, rattled off the plate number for the truck. She heard the sound of fingers tapping on the other line. Before he'd finished, though, she quickly added. "Also, should mention, don't let this show up anywhere traceable. Probably best no one knows what I'm looking for."

He snorted. "I'm working private security in South America. Not exactly swimming in red tape down here. If I wanted to, I could fly a helicopter into the president's house, and they wouldn't blink." Then, his tone shifted. "Stolen truck," he said. "Big black thing, that the one?"

"Yeah..." Cora trailed off, frowning. "Anything else besides it being stolen?"

"Nu-huh. Owner was shot at the scene. Three days ago. What are you involved in?"

"I didn't shoot him."

"Uh-huh."

"Johnny. I mean it. I didn't shoot him."

"Of course."

She sighed. She could tell he wasn't so sure. But she didn't have time to convince him of this. And so, instead, she said, "Alright—so I got something else then. Forget the plates. I figured they'd be a dead end. I want to know about a golden snake."

"That a euphemism?"

"Har. Har. No, it was on a briefcase. Looked like an S, with a red eye like a ruby."

"And what am I looking *in.*"

Cora sighed, considering it, then said, "Suspected traffickers. Drug dealers. International cartels. The like."

More typing sounds. She waited now, walking in the night-time breeze, shivering a bit now as she moved into the night. She was now far enough away from the crime scene that she decided it would be safe enough to call a taxi.

She cycled to the app on her phone while Johnny continued to work in the background. A few more minutes passed though, before he said. "Got it. Yeah, looking at it now. So, we've got three options. Chinese mob, working primarily in Beijing."

"Nope."

"Hmm. Well, we got a golden snake emblem for a shell company suspected to be associated with Rhode Island organized crime. And then..." A pause. "Yeah, Colombian cartel."

"That last one," Cora said quickly. "Send me the picture, will you."

No sooner had she made the request, had her phone buzzed. She glanced down at the attached picture in the message. Her eyebrows lifted slowly. It matched. The same golden snake she'd seen on the briefcase.

"What is it?" she said.

"Umm...warehouse," he replied after a moment. "Looks like nothing is confirmed, but DEA has some eyes on the place. Pretty quiet for the last couple years...but there was an issue where they found a man working for the company with a big stash of narcotics in his tires."

"Company name? Oh, wait, never mind. I see it." She frowned at the logo he'd sent, staring at the golden lettering beneath the golden emblem. *Gild & Sundry.*

She wrinkled her nose, frowning. "What are they supposed to be involved in?"

"That's part of the issue," he replied. "Nothing clear on the books. Technically, a shipping company, but their tax info is spotty at best. IRS is looking at an audit. But...you know places like this..."

"A shell within a shell," she replied, nodding slowly. "Reminds me of the UAE. Remember that banker?"

"Huh, yeah," Johnny chuckled.

And for a moment, it almost felt good-natured. But then, both of them, realizing they were letting their guards down, cleared their throats awkwardly.

"I—well, thanks Johnny. You got an address for the place."

"Umm, yeah, yeah. Gotta be going myself. Here, sending you the warehouse. It's a state over from where you are."

"I didn't tell you where I was."

"Nah. Psh. Think that's gonna stop me? That all Cobra, or you want to reminisce some more?"

She hung up this time.

And, admittedly, it felt good.

There was something just so... pleased with itself about Johnny. She shook her head, glaring into the night. Once upon a time, she'd found him charming.

Now...

She sighed, closed her eyes, and tried not to allow her mind to wander too far afield.

She checked her phone for an update from the taxi app, waiting on the curb, and listening to the sounds of the night. Her screen brightened, the device buzzing as Johnny sent her the address for the warehouse.

She studied the information, feeling a sense of inevitability. She was in too deep now to back out. Besides, she still had to make sure those cops in Westville got more than a hand and leg shot. If they were looking the other way while girls from single-parent families were kidnapped, she'd be happy to see the whole station burned down.

She scowled, exhaled, and sent a quick follow-up message to Saul about the audio recording. "Captain and officers from Westville police station," she texted quickly. "Dirty. Deal with."

Then she lowered her phone again, considering her next move.

A warehouse associated with the same company the man in the expensive suit was from.

Now that she thought of it, the road they'd fled on would take them in the same direction as the warehouse. She frowned, and then reached a decision.

It wasn't like there was any reason to head back to West Virginia anyhow.

Besides, things with the cops in Westville could easily escalate. It

86

was probably best she wasn't readily locatable.

She waited, watching for the taxi. Part of her wished she'd stayed long enough to keep one of the guns she'd snatched at the police station. But in her haste to beat a retreat, she'd left the firearm on the premises. No sense carrying around a weapon used to shoot public servants.

She wasn't certain *what* she was doing, but she did know that one way or another, she needed to find that man with the golden chain.

Either willingly...

Or very, very painfully...

He'd lead her to Caitlin.

And anyone else standing in her way?

It wouldn't be pretty.

CHAPTER THIRTEEN

Cora watched from the vantage point overlooking the small compound. The warehouse was situated off a desert road, at the end of a switchback, hidden from the highway or any prying eyes. A row of barbed wire topped a gate, only further serving to isolate the lonely warehouse.

Trucks carrying shipping containers occasionally came and went.

Odd, since there were no ships, or even large bodies of water, for hundreds of miles.

Cora maintained her prone posture, resting amidst dust and scrubby vegetation. The taxi had taken her to the nearest town. Hoofing it had brought her the rest of the way.

And now, the collar of her shirt lifted to help her breath despite the dust, she watched the movement patterns of the guards.

Men with guns.

Too many men for a shipping warehouse.

No sign of the man with the golden chain yet, though. She didn't have binoculars, and wished she'd been able to get some sort of aerial footage.

But now, working without the seal of approval from the American government, she supposed she'd simply have to make do with what she had.

She huffed in frustration, wishing that she'd also brought a weapon.

She'd thought she was coming to a funeral, though, not a livewire mission into the arms of a waiting army.

She'd already counted seven armed men. Their weapons were hidden, for the most part. But who was there to hide them from, out here, in the desert?

They clearly didn't know they were being watched, and yet they moved with precision, with great care. Not military training, but rather a different type of training, a darker sort of experience.

She kept her attention fixated on them, looking for a flaw in their movement patterns. Currently, she was specifically eyeballing two men in blue uniforms and gray hats with golden snakes on the brims. They were moving around the side of the warehouse, eyes forward. No chatting, no small talk. One of the men, earlier, had taken a smoke break, but had done it out of the line of sight from the cameras dotting the place.

She exhaled slowly, feeling the warmth of her breath against the cupped hem of her shirt.

The sun was bright, high in the sky, watching her where she lay. She'd managed to get a few hours of sleep in the ride from Westville, but now she was holding back a yawn. Still, while she normally would have waited until evening, the hornet's nest she'd kicked up back at the police station suggested the sooner she pulled these threads, the better.

Already, she'd received phone calls from both the director and from Agent Brady. Whether they wanted to know about the recording she'd sent or wanted to discuss the charges being brought against her, she didn't know, nor did she care.

Now, she faced a mission.

There was something exhilarating, almost relieving about finding herself face-to-face with a virtual army.

An impossible problem.

Impossible, though, was the fun part.

And so, she slipped back, keeping low until she was no longer within the view of the compound. Then she pushed to her feet, shook the dust from her hands, checked the utility knife in her pocket, and broke into a jog, head low under the sun. She would need to grab some water soon. She also would have to pay close attention to her own temperature.

In her experience, the quickest way for missions like this to go sideways was to neglect the simple things.

It was in the details that a mission would succeed or fail.

As she moved down the trail, considering her options, she wondered if a phone call to Brady was in order. But no, the FBI had been clear where she was concerned.

If they found out where she was and what she was up to, chances were a prison sentence would have her name on it. And so, waving the dust from her face and lowering her collar, she moved towards the portion of fence where she'd spotted a small blind spot from the guards and cameras. She moved slower now, cautious, not wanting to catch any eye before she was close enough to breach the fence.

She steadied herself, taking a quick breath.

Cora watched through the gaps in the fence, waiting for the two men with the gray caps to continue their circuit around the side of the rectangular, white building. Once she spotted the backs of their heels, she took this as her cue. Her fingers found the mesh, pulling taut on the wire. She made it halfway up, and then removed the sweater she had borrowed from Jamie. Using this, she flung it over the top of the fence.

She scrambled up the rest of the way, moving with practiced precision, the muscles in her arms straining. Where her arms extended ahead of her, no longer wearing long sleeves, she spotted the many tattoos, including the one of the cobra on her right forearm. There were scars too. She spotted the two white marks on her left bicep. Gunshot wounds. There was a knife wound on her shoulder, which she couldn't currently see.

To her, sometimes it felt as if she had already lived multiple lives.

She reached the top of the fence, slowly, quietly pushing the loops of barbed wire to the side as best she could. This was the benefit of being slim. The sweater was used to block one side of the adjusted wire. Then, she moved up the fence, through the wire, hung for a second, wincing where her pants leg caught on a barb. Carefully, using her abdominal muscles, she removed her leg from the hook of metal, and dropped to the ground.

Her foot caught a discarded glass bottle, sending it skittering. She winced against the noise. The small, concrete curb at the base of the fence had blocked the bottle from sight. But now, as she scanned the ground, she noticed multiple bottles and a few cigarettes.

Clearly, the blind spot wasn't unfamiliar to the guards.

Which meant she couldn't stay long. She reached up, snatched the sleeve of her sweater, shook it a bit to dislodge it, and then put it back on.

All of it had taken a minute.

Which meant she had thirty seconds before the two guards circled around the east side of the building again. They would see her.

She kept low, in a crouch, hastening towards the side of the big building.

As she did, she heard a sudden rattle. Voices. She tensed. She glanced back, and realized a large truck was being brought through the sliding gate outside the warehouse.

She frowned at the truck. Another shipping container.

But was it common for shipping containers to have breathing holes?

She couldn't be sure, but strange perforations along the metal certainly caught her attention.

90

She frowned, watching as the truck was wheeled towards one of the loading docks.

Then she heard footsteps. The guards were drawing near.

She lingered for a moment, considering her options, but then, keeping low, she moved directly under a westward=facing security camera. Again, it wouldn't be able to see her unless she moved two feet to the left.

She hotfooted and reached the opposite side of the warehouse just in time, slipping around the edge of the building as she heard the voices of the two men come around the corner.

She rested, back flat against the warehouse building. Now, on this side, there were two more guards. But they were in a small garage, and she had spotted them working on a jeep

Another two guards stood stationed by the doors of the warehouse. And one guard remained by the exit, which was only accessible if she turned the corner of the building one more time.

She wanted to enter the warehouse to find the man with the golden chain. He was the liaison for the police back in Westville. He was the one who had bribed them. If anyone knew where Caitlin Johnson was, it would be him, but as of yet, she had not set eyes on him.

She considered her options, and then realized what she had to do. A Trojan horse. If she wanted to enter the compound, then the truck, the loading docks would be the necessary disturbance she needed.

She sighed in frustration as this realization struck her; it meant she would have to backtrack, heading the other way.

And so, she waited, quietly listening to the voices, the crunch of footsteps.

She heard the men drawing near.

She would have to be fast. Non-lethal. So far, all the guys stood guilty of was dealing with a criminal boss. Besides, she wasn't in the business of stabbing people needlessly—she tensed, braced against the wall. The small garage, with the two other guards faced her. But, from her vantage point on the cliff, when analyzing the warehouse, she had noticed the guards occupied by the jeep. She would have to trust her luck held out. If they spotted her and raised an alarm, then there was a good chance this warehouse would also serve as her grave.

She kept quiet, waiting, patient, listening. The voices were near. Certainly not English. Spanish?

She couldn't pick it out until she spotted a foot move around the corner two feet from where she pressed. She stared at the booted foot, tense, hand cupped. And then the man that belonged to that foot followed.

As he emerged, he went still and blinked. That was all he had time for. Her hand shot out, her thumb going directly into his neck. The jutting digit found soft skin. At the same time, she couldn't wait for the second guard around the corner. She cursed, and darted forward, using the motion of her flinging arm to pivot around the wall.

The second man was a few steps back, and it took her a moment to realize what had caught his attention.

Blood streaking the wall. She frowned, and realized, in a horrible moment, that her leg was bleeding from the barbed wire. No time to think about it. No time to tend an injury. The man started to shout as he spotted her coming over the crumpling form of his gurgling companion. And so, she went for the throat a second time.

If he screamed, alerted the rest of them, then five men with guns would be hunting her. Not to mention whoever was still inside the warehouse.

She brought her knuckles into his throat. The scream cut off into a wheeze. She then followed up with a quick knee to the groin.

His hand had barely even reached for his holster by the time he was moaning and toppling. She kicked him in the head for good measure as he fell.

It was like stomping cantaloupe.

Unconscious the instant she connected.

She turned her attention to the second man, who was still grabbing at his throat, gasping, but at the same time, reaching desperately for his weapon.

"I'll take that," she murmured. She reached down, took the weapon from him, and used the butt of the gun to strike the man on the temple. He also slumped to the ground.

Breathing heavily, she considered hiding the bodies.

It would take some time before they recovered their senses. So, she grabbed the second gun from the second guard, deciding that if they woke up in the next few minutes, at least they wouldn't be armed. There was no time for anything else; she was playing a game of cat and mouse. If anyone spotted her, the game was over. And if she lost, she could only really think of one outcome.

She was moving again, one gun tucked in her waistband, the other clutched in her hand.

She reached the edge of the warehouse near the loading dock, listening intently. Cora shot a glance back towards where she had left the two unconscious guards. No one had raised an alarm. No sign that the men in the garage had seen anything.

But something she did hear made her skin crawl.

The echoing, tinny sound of *crying*.

At first, she wasn't sure what she was listening to. But after a few moments, she realized that it was weeping. And it was coming from inside the shipping container.

She felt her skin crawl. She heard barking voices, yelling. She risked a glance around the edge of the warehouse, hopeful that the distraction of the large truck would obscure her.

And as she watched, attentive, she realized that three more men had emerged from inside the warehouse. One of them was pounding his fist against the side of the shipping container, and then chuckling when he received more fearful sobbing. Another was barking instructions, shouting in a strong accent, "Shut up and follow me!"

The exit to the container was out of sight, currently perched in the warehouse dock. But the loading zone was also serving as a walkway for someone she recognized.

Her eyes narrowed as they landed on the man from last night. At least, she assumed it was him. She hadn't gotten a particularly good look at his face. But he was wearing the same gold chain, and a day-old suit.

The expensive suit wasn't nearly as pressed as it had been the night before; it looked a little worn, sweat-stained, and slept in.

But it was the same suit, nonetheless. And, when he spoke, she recognized the smooth, velvety voice. "Put them with the others," he said. "Make sure to clean out the container before sending it back. Rall, if I hear you skip the cleaning, I'll cut you to pieces."

The calm way in which he issued the threat sent prickles along her skin; she could hear the sobbing fading now. The sounds of voices being ushered into the warehouse.

She continued to listen and watch.

But once the man with the golden chain had said his piece, he turned to head back into the warehouse. As he pivoted, she cursed and ducked out of sight.

For a moment, he had glanced directly at her.

She remained motionless, pressed against the wall.

There were three men by the truck—all of them armed. The problem about taking a shot at them was the risk of hitting someone in that shipping container.

So, she waited, breathing slowly. Her aversion to shooting these men, though, had quickly dissipated. It was one thing in self-defense to shoot corrupt cops. Another thing entirely to stage a sort of mission, shooting foreign nationals on American soil. Then again, she had known what she was getting into. It would have been dishonest to pretend otherwise.

She gripped her weapon, tense. Then she heard a whispered instruction. The prickles along her arm moved to her neck.

The whisper grew louder. She heard, "Find out what's taking the two of them. We need help in here. Rall, grab them. And remember what I said about cleaning the container. I mean it."

It took her a moment, but then she heard the sound of approaching footsteps, suggesting that the man was drawing near.

Cora waited, poised. Then, at the last minute, she slipped her gun into her waistband and pulled out her utility knife, flipping it open with a practiced motion and a deft flick of her thumb.

She waited a second. The footsteps approached. The sounds from the shipping container had ceased. But the haunting resonance of those sobs remained. The earlier sense of proportionality had been replaced by a grim, just sense of vindication.

She waited as a shadow crossed in front of her. A pause, the grinding sound of a foot shifting on asphalt. A response, this time coming from inside the warehouse by the sound of things.

A dark muttered comment as the man named Rall turned the corner. This time, she didn't go to him but rather grabbed his collar and pulled him to her.

The man tasked to clean out the shipping container full of sobbing humans, who had been pounding his fist against the corrugated metal to elicit their tears, didn't have a chance to cry out. He tried, but she moved too quickly. Her knife flashed, buried in his neck, and then withdrew.

He stared at her, bug-eyed, red suddenly pouring down his neck. She held him upright for a second, and then tugged him to the ground, pivoting to avoid the blood from sloshing onto her clothing.

And then she stepped over him, moving quickly.

The truck driver didn't notice her, but she saw the way he was tapping his fingers against the steering wheel, humming to himself. Clearly, he had no concern about what was transpiring in the back of his cargo container.

She took rapid footsteps. The second guard who'd been unloading the shipping container suddenly emerged around the front of the truck. She hadn't spotted his movement but had assumed he had returned inside the warehouse along with the boss.

She froze. He cursed. He pulled his gun. She flung her knife.

It buried in his neck.

Suddenly, the driver in the truck glanced over, eyes suddenly flaring as he watched the man topple to the ground, choking on his own blood.

Cora was moving again, though. She reached the truck door before he could lock it, yanking it open. Her gun was now in her hand, pointing inside. "Shout and I shoot you," she said firmly. "You understand me?"

A man with olive skin and dark hair above long eyelashes nodded quickly. She pointed her gun at his head. "Hands up, away from the steering wheel."

He instantly complied, and by the continued silence, no one else had spotted her. She kept her gun pointed at him, and said in a whisper, "How many people were in that container?"

He winced, shaking his head, and tapping an ear.

She repeated, "How many?" She held up a hand, cycling through different numbers.

He nodded and held up all ten of his fingers.

"Who are they?"

He winced and shrugged. He said something in a language she didn't know.

"Where are you from?"

He stared at her, panicked. Trembling.

"Where?" She tried again. She tapped her finger to her chest. "America." She pointed at him.

His eyes widened in recognition. "Columbia," he said simply.

She nodded slowly. "Who do you work for? What is this outfit?"

He winced, shaking his head.

She was growing frustrated now. She gestured at him and muttered urgently. "Come to me, across the seats."

This time, he seemed to understand what she meant, judging by her gestures alone.

Hesitantly, he slid across the seat divide, hands shaking as he moved.

When he reached her, her hand lashed out, grabbed him, and pulled him hard from inside the cabin. As he fell with a yelp, her clenched fist gripping the butt of the gun lashed out.

A dull *thunk*. And then he hit the ground like a sack of potatoes.

Three men unconscious. Two bleeding out.

She had counted seven guards in total. But at least two of them had come from inside the warehouse. Which meant, there were still four left. The two in the garage. The one by the exit door. And then, where was the—

The sudden sound of gunfire. The glass window above her shattered as bullets slammed into the metal truck door.

Something hot zipped across her arm. She cursed, moving quickly.

It took her a second, but she spotted the shooter, standing by the gates where he had allowed the truck entrance.

Her gun was raised.

The man was shouting something.

He shot at her again. This time, the headlights smashed. Small particles of glass sprayed across her skin. But she fired back. Two shots. Missed. He was taking refuge behind a guardhouse by the gate.

She waited, timing, exhaling slowly. Her arm extended in front of her, muscles taut, gun steady.

He looked up, she fired.

He went down again. This time he wouldn't rise.

And now, she was moving fast. Everyone would have heard that.

CHAPTER FOURTEEN

A shout alerted her to trouble. The man who had been guarding the exit door emerged around the warehouse. She dropped him with two gunshots.

Cora kept moving. She vaulted onto the loading dock platform and then rushed under the raised metal door.

Voices were shouting from inside now. Two men with guns were cursing, sprinting in the direction of an office door in the back of the warehouse. One of them turned to fire. She shot him twice, his arms flung out as his weapon went flying. The other man cursed, dropped his weapon, and raised his hands.

She gestured for him to get on the ground. He didn't. She aimed and said, "*Down.*"

He complied, face first, hands flat against the smooth floor.

She hastened forward, kicking the gun out of the way and quickly scanning the warehouse. There was a loft section up a metal ladder. She couldn't hear the sound of whimpering voices anymore, and so she raced towards the door and paused, pressing her cheek against the metal.

She could hear crying now. Frightened voices.

She tried the door handle. *Locked.*

She cursed, pointing at the man on the ground. "Where's the key?"

The prostrate man shook his head. "Where is the *key*?" she snapped.

Before he could reply, the exit door burst open. Two more gunmen. Coming from the garage.

She turned, dropped to a knee. Fired twice more. She caught both of them in the chest. They collapsed backwards, falling through the exit door. A fire alarm was now blaring; the voices from inside the metal door rising in volume and panic.

By her account, there were no more guards. But the man with the golden chain was nowhere to be found. She glanced up at the loft section and spotted a small office with glass windows and foam paneling.

She cold-cocked the man on the ground, knocking him out as well.

Soon, the ones she had put unconscious outside would start to regain their senses. She had to move.

She hastened to the metal ladder, flinging herself up it, her gun striking against the rungs. She paused halfway, checking the clip. She cursed, wiped off the handle on her shirt, smudging any fingerprints, and then tossed the gun off into the corner. She pulled the second weapon from her waistband, checked it, and then continued up the ladder. As she emerged, a shotgun blast nearly took her head off her shoulders.

She ducked just in time. Shot skimmed off the metal floor, in an eruption of sparks.

Cora cursed under her breath, waited, and then heard a voice call down from the loft, "I don't know who you are, but I'll pay double whatever you're being offered if you show me your hands, and tell me who employed you!"

Cora braced against the ladder, one shoulder wedged against the second rung.

She gripped her gun, fingers tight. There was another sudden blast—more sparks erupted off the top of the platform. By the sound of things, the man was using a shotgun.

"Are you with Giuliano?" He called.

She didn't reply.

He spoke in his native language. And though Cora didn't understand, she could tell there was an inflection of a question.

Again, she remained quiet. Across from her, she spotted movement through the metal walkway, occasional slits in the structure caused shadows to pass through when the figure above moved over them.

She could hear the footsteps clinking against the metal as he drew nearer. If she allowed him to get on top of her, it would be a coin flip to see who got their shot off first. Granted, judging by his aim, she would have taken those odds.

But she had a better idea.

Hastily, she holstered her weapon in her waistband. And then she released the rung of the ladder and grabbed the support bars beneath the small metal platform.

Like a child on monkey bars at the park, she swung from one to the next, moving as quietly as she could; she tracked the sound of footsteps, of motion. "At least tell me your name!" the man above said, his voice not as calm as it was before. Instead of smooth and velvety, he sounded panicked. "Impressive. You killed my men. I could make you rich, you know."

She kept swinging on the metal support bars and reached the opposite side of the platform. Quietly, she climbed up.

She peered through the rail and watched as the man in the suit reached the ladder. He gripped a shotgun—a twelve-gauge—waited a second, asked another question, and then suddenly darted forward, aiming and firing.

The gunshot blast reverberated.

But again, she used the cover of the noise to quickly hop onto the metal platform, raise her gun, pointing it at his back, and then said, clearly, "If you don't drop that I'll kill you."

It wasn't ominous, and she didn't lower her voice to sound scarier. Instead, she let the truth of the words carry the threat.

The man with the shotgun tensed.

"If you twitch in my direction," she said, quietly, "I'll do to you what I've done to all your soldiers."

There was a faint little gasp. A swallow. And then the twelve-gauge clattered to the ground.

"Hands up and keep your eyes forward!"

He kept his hands down, though.

For a moment, his left hand was out of sight by his waist.

She took a few steps to the side, and said, quietly, "If you pull that gun in your waistband, I'll shoot you dead."

He froze.

And only then, very reluctantly, did his hands find the sky.

He turned just as slowly, glaring at her, his eyes full of contempt.

She stared back. And for the first time, she was given a good look at the man with the soft voice.

There was something almost feminine about his features. He was clearly a man, but pretty. He had smooth, perfectly moisturized olive skin. Eyebrows hunched and plucked as if he was constantly in a state of surprise.

His tongue wet his lips, and he shifted uncomfortably from one foot to the other. "I don't know you," he said, slowly.

"No, I didn't expect you to. Now you're going to move down that ladder and unlock the door with the girls in it. But first, I need you to pull that weapon out with your left hand and lower it to the ground. Then kick it towards me."

It took a few moments, but then, with a heavy sigh, he nodded, reached into his waistband, removed his weapon, and slowly lowered it.

And then, at another gesture of her weapon, he kicked it towards her. "Now head down the ladder. No quick movements. And if you try to run—"

"Yes, yes, you'll *kill* me. I heard you the first time."

Cora nodded once. She didn't blink, watching him closely as he reluctantly approached the ladder and began to descend. As they moved down the ladder, Cora pulled her phone from her pocket. She hastily dialed a number, put it on speaker, and listened as it connected. She turned away from the ladder, gun still pointed towards the man in the suit. He already had a key in hand and was approaching the locked storage door with stiff movements.

Two things pulled on Cora's attention: the frightened sounds from the room and the ring tone of her phone.

Composed again, the figure with the golden chain unlocked the door, then stepped stiffly aside.

A bright light illuminated ten figures huddled together against the far wall.

Their faces streaked, stained with dirt and sweat. Their clothing old and foul.

Ten women, all shaking, stared at Cora.

She glared at the man by the door. "What is *this*?"

He glanced at her and pursed his lips. He just gave a noncommittal shrug.

Of course, Cora had suspected trafficking all along. But seeing it in its sordid details, her stomach turned.

She realized a few of the women were staring at the gun in her hand, their eyes open in horror.

She quickly called out, "I'm here to help you. It's going to be fine. I promise."

Suddenly, she heard a voice on the end of the line. Her phone call had connected. For a brief instant, she was distracted. She glanced at the women in the room. "Caitlin Johnson? Caitlin?"

But as she scanned the women in the container, she felt a sinking sensation. Her friend's daughter wasn't here. None of the women matched the picture that Jamie had provided her. None of them reacted to the name she was calling.

She felt a jolt of anger, accompanying grief. She tried to keep her tone steady, even. In moments like these, victims didn't need her grief. They needed her leadership. They needed to know someone was there to help.

And so, she said, firmly, her voice steady, "Help is on the way. I promise. Just stay there."

The women didn't look so scared now. A few of them were murmuring and whispering to each other.

Only now did Cora react to the voice chirping over her phone. She raised the device, turned off the speaker, and said, "Saul? I'm going to need your help."

Agent Brady replied quickly. "Cora, what's going on? What was that audio you sent me? Those police officers, they're saying that someone who fit your description threatened them. Shot them."

Cora blinked under the deluge of information. But then, she said, "So you did send someone to speak with them?"

Agent Brady said, "I'm here myself, Cora. What's going on?"

"You're in Westville, Colorado?"

"I just arrived. Now are you going to tell me what's happening? What's that sound in the background?"

She ignored this part of the question. Instead, she said, "All right, Saul, listen closely. Those cops are corrupt. Dirty. They were taking bribes to look the other way so traffickers could pick off some of the more vulnerable members of the town. I am currently looking for one of those women."

There was a slow, steady exhale. Agent Brady wasn't normally one given to histrionics. He said, carefully, "Cora, you know you don't work for the FBI, yes? Whatever you're doing, you know—"

"Did you tell the deputy director?"

"I haven't had time to talk with anyone. I came here based on an anonymous tip."

Cora felt a jolt of gratitude. "You might want to keep it that way, Saul. Because I have something else. There's a warehouse about four hours from where you are; there are ten women in here."

"Ten? Victims?"

"They're going to need help. I can't stay, for obvious reasons. Plus," she said and winced. "There's a few bodies. I'll be tying up some of them but the others," she said, with a faint wince, "probably are going to need some body bags."

"Jesus Christ, Cora, what are you doing?"

"Brady, do you want to help these women or not?"

A faint huff of air, and then, the older, veteran of the FBI muttered, "Of course. Tell me where to find them."

"Perfect. I'm texting you the address. Good luck, Saul."

"Wait, Cora, don't hang—"

She hung up.

Then, she pointed her gun once more at the man with the golden chain. "Food? Water? Where?"

He hesitated briefly and swallowed. "What?"

She didn't repeat the question but did wave her gun.

"Upstairs," he said hurriedly.

Cora nodded, gesturing at the two women closest to the door. The way they had postured themselves, protectively around the others, she decided these were the ones she wanted to speak with. "Did you hear that? Food, water. Police are going to be on the way. They'll have ways to help you guys. I'm very sorry. If it's any consolation, some of the guys who had a hand in this have already paid."

Then, quickly, though it pained her not to give further instruction, she directed her attention towards the trafficker. "You're going to help me tie up a few of those unconscious soldiers. And then you're coming with me."

"What?" He stammered.

"Not so suave now? What? *What*? That's going to be *my* question. For now, you better just do what I say. Clear?"

Then, before he had time to protest or react, she snapped, "Now get moving. Today's going to be a long day for you!"

Caitlin Johnson was not in this warehouse. But this man, this place, everything she'd seen proved one thing. This guy knew where Caitlin was.

And willingly or not, he was going to take Cora to her.

CHAPTER FIFTEEN

In the distance, Cora could hear sirens rapidly approaching and thought she heard the sound of helicopter blades against the horizon. She had to hand it to Agent Brady. He'd managed to get tactical to move quick.

But now, she didn't linger to watch. A cloud of dust kicked up behind them as she sped away on the desert road. Tires squealed as she turned sharply, moving at a breakneck pace in the opposite direction of the compound. Having secured the surviving soldiers and liberated the captive women, Cora was now focused on the next task.

But in order to find Caitlin, she was going to need the man in her back seat to start talking. His hands were bound behind him as she hadn't buckled him in.

As she swerved sharply again, tires squealing, he yelled, flying across the seat, his head thumping into the door.

He groaned in pain, trying to speak to protest, but she swerved the other way. In the rearview mirror, she spotted where snakes of black stained the asphalt. Where the dust turned up, rising in a cloud. The sound of sirens in the distance only added to the chaos.

As she sped away from the compound, she could feel her nerves quieting, could feel her mind focusing.

She *had* to find where Caitlin was.

Before it was too late.

She shouted now, swerving once more, but then straightening out in order to give him a chance to hear the question. "Where is Caitlin Johnson? The girl you took from Westville. Two months ago. Where is she?"

The man in the backseat was groaning. He stammered, "You're going to break my arms."

Every time she veered one way or the other, his hands, bound behind his back, would slam against the seat and the door. Bracing himself, his arms would twist at an odd angle. She wanted to summon compassion but was finding it very difficult.

"That is not an answer to my question!"

"No, no, wait, wait!" His eyes widened as he watched her hands begin to twist the steering wheel again.

She steadied, waiting.

He screeched, "I don't know who you're talking about! No, really, I don't—"

Another squeal of the tires, this time taking a curve with a posted speed limit of 35 mph. She was going 80.

The trafficker screamed but then slammed into the opposite door, thrown across the seats.

Something *cracked*. For his sake, she hoped it was just the plastic covering on the door, and not one of his bones.

"Stop!" he yelled, his voice pleading. "I'm begging you, stop!"

"Begging now? Is that what they did? And did you stop? No? Didn't think so—now tell me, where is Caitlin?" her eyes flashed in the rearview mirror, and she added, "I can do this all day!"

They continued to tear through the desert road, under the bright sun, leaving a trail of dust and rubber.

The man, shaking badly now, was muttering under his breath.

She straightened again on the road.

Through tight lips, she growled, "Just so we're both on the same page, the next thing I do is slam on the brakes. I want you to consider, for a moment, what's going to happen if I do that. Imagine your body, like a rag doll, flying across the seats. Imagine your head colliding with the windshield, maybe the head rest of the other chair. Do you think your neck will snap? You think something will break?" She spoke conversationally, somewhat channeling the voice he had used back at the police station. The voice of someone who knew they were in control.

He was stammering horribly, shaking his head, his olive skin turning pale as the blood left his cheeks. But then, at last, he blurted out, "Don't-don't do that. I don't know where this woman is. But I know who does!"

"Talk faster!" As she said it, she floored the gas. He started speaking more rapidly. "I work for a man only known as the Merchant. He's Greek. Look, he doesn't tell me where he takes them. I'm just the middleman. I'm a victim too!"

"The Merchant? What's his real name?"

A note of panic, joining the rapid prattle, "I don't know. If I knew, I swear, I would tell you!"

"And what is he going to do with Caitlin?" Cora said, her voice shaking. "Where would he take her?"

Another pained gasp, a shaking head. "I don't know," he moaned like a petulant child. "If I did, I would tell you. But I don't. You have to believe me."

Cora had to do no such thing.

She studied him a moment longer in the rearview mirror and then reached a decision. "Hold on," she said, sardonically. And then, as he shouted in protest, she slammed on the brakes.

The man shot forward, his head slamming into the back of her chair. He tried to absorb the blow on his shoulder, but only ended up twisting his body into an odd shape.

As their car skidded, tires squealing, he collapsed into the back seat, suddenly silent.

She sat in the car, idling on the desert road, her chest throbbing from where the seatbelt had squeezed at the sudden stop.

She glanced back, breathing heavily, extended a hand and felt no pulse.

Adrenaline coursed through her system. She checked more closely, turning so she could extend her arm fully. She found a pulse.

She wasn't sure if this should be a relief or a disappointment.

But for now, the trafficker was unconscious. She would have to place another call to Saul.

Because she certainly wasn't going to carry him any further. A couple of hours on the side of the road in the desert heat might give the man a new perspective on jamming women into shipping containers like sardines.

But as she kicked open her door, slipping around the side to busy herself with pulling him out of the back, she placed a call.

It took a few moments, but then, the call connected.

"Haven't fallen in love with me again, have you?" came the cheeky reply.

She scowled, and in normal situations might have hung up at just that offense. But this wasn't a normal predicament. "Johnny," she snapped, "I don't have time for your lip. What do you know about a trafficker named the Merchant? Apparently, he's Greek."

"Wait, shit, for real, *the* Merchant?"

"You know him?" She said, excited.

"No. Just playing. Look, Cora, I can't be your guy in the chair. I have my own job to do."

"At least this time I don't hear gunshots in the background."

"No, true. I suspect if I had called you a couple of hours ago, I very well might have."

She frowned, wrinkling her nose, "Are you tracking my phone?"

"No. But I did have a couple of feelers out on that warehouse you asked about last night. Doesn't sound like it had a very good morning."

"No, I suppose they didn't."

She reached the back seat, inhaling the warm, dusty air. She pulled open the door, and then dragged the trafficker out of the seat, depositing him onto the side of the road, pushing him, with her foot, off the asphalt. If she had been in a particularly vindictive mood, she might have just left him in the middle-of-the-road.

"I need you to place a call to the police about one of the traffickers. I think I found him."

"Found him, right. He still have his fingernails?"

"He's fine. Getting some beauty sleep."

"I take it you're not just calling to brag about clunking some scumbag."

"The day I call you to brag," Cora said, her voice a growl, "is the day you can take me out back and shoot me."

"Are you asking me to take you out?"

"Johnny, this is something I wish I'd said when we were dating. You're not funny."

"Now, see, Cora, your memory is failing you. You did tell me that when we were dating. Multiple times."

She inhaled shakily, again, resisting the urge to hang up; sometimes, one couldn't choose their allies. And now, things were urgent. "The Merchant, Johnny, I need you to—"

"Just did. Give me a second, I'm tracking his yacht."

"His what?"

"The guy has a yacht," Johnny said, with a grunt. "Also, he is Turkish. He says he is Greek, for business reasons, kind of like that yogurt guy."

"What?"

"Right, he's right below Florida. Looks like he's been there a couple of days, going back and forth between some ports. Listed as a pleasure trip. He has clearance. What do you expect to find on that yacht?"

"I didn't know there was going to be a yacht. Crap. Johnny, in that case, I have another favor to ask you."

"Should I be keeping a running tally or just consider this a charitable donation?"

"Consider it what you want, but a woman's life is on the line. That guy who used to charter planes out of here for drug smugglers—you still have his number?"

"I wouldn't lose a number like that. Skyler is a character. Why?"

Cora sighed. She didn't like the way he had said *character*. But she pressed on, "I'm going to need a flight. Tonight. And I need you to keep me up-to-date on that yacht; tell me if it goes to port."

"Cora, now hang on one moment. I'm not working for you. A couple of favors doesn't mean you can—"

Now she hung up. And boy, it felt satisfying.

CHAPTER SIXTEEN

Cora sprinted across the tarmac, holding a hand to her face, one arm braced against the wind churned by the helicopter blades. Blinking red and green lights, beneath the body of the black machine illuminated the helicopter pad. The private airfield was motionless in the dead of night.

Cora had to hand it to Johnny's contact. The man was punctual, at the very least. The spray-painted cartoon of a woman clad in a skimpy bikini staining the side of the helicopter, though, was somewhat less impressive.

She reached the side of the helicopter, holding up three fingers the way Johnny had told her to. She then cleared her voice and shouted the passcode Johnny had given, "The sailor sobs at noon!"

The door to the helicopter kicked open. A man was sitting there. A man she hadn't quite been expecting. For one, he wore a straw bonnet, with headphones perched over it. For another, he was completely tan, but unnaturally so, and, judging by some of the patches of pale skin, he had used a spray.

And the reason she knew he was tan was because he was wearing nothing except for bright, pink underwear. The rest of his clothing, by the looks of it, was drying in the backseat. She stared at the half naked man in the sun bonnet and wondered exactly what she had gotten herself into.

But the man was beaming at her, gesturing.

She paused, and stared at her hand, holding three fingers, and then stared at the headphones accompanying the wild whooping sound of the helicopter blades. There was no way he had heard what she'd said.

Slowly, she lowered her hand, her eyes narrowing suspiciously. The password she'd been given by Johnny had seemed a bit much. And now, she was starting to suspect that had been more for her ex-boyfriend's amusement than anything the pilot had requested.

For all he knew, she was a federal agent coming to arrest him. But he greeted her with a grin and a wave.

"Johnny told you I was coming, right?" She called out.

The man tapped his headphones and shook his head. He gestured again for her to get in.

"You know where we're headed, yeah?"

Another big grin and adjustment.

She sighed faintly.

Then, the man extended a second pair of headphones.

The wild churning of the helicopter blades was making it nearly impossible to hear anything. So, reluctantly, she slipped into the front seat, heart pounding. She shot a look over her shoulder at the rest of the airfield; no sign that anyone was coming towards them. No sign that the police had managed to catch up with her. At this point, she didn't doubt that people were starting to look for her.

A few phone calls from Agent Brady, but she had put her device on silent.

Part of her was wondering if she ought to just block his number. Then again, she was going to need him for what came next.

She slipped into the helicopter, put on the headphones, slammed the door, and said, "Are you Skyler?"

"What?" He said, and then held up a finger. He flipped the switch on the dashboard. Then said, "Are you Cobra?"

She glared. "That's right. Skyler Brodrick?"

He chuckled. "I guess so. I forgot I changed it."

She wasn't at all sure what that meant.

Then, still cheerful, his voice echoing in the way it might over a recording device, he said, "I hear you need some help,"

"Johnny sent the coordinates?"

"Some yacht, out at sea. That right?"

She nodded again. But he wasn't watching, flipping more buttons. And then, his hand moved to what she could only describe as a joystick between them. They began to rise and she tensed.

"You know how to land wet?" He asked.

Cora realized Johnny must have not told him much about her. Otherwise, he would have known the question was somewhat offensive to a branch of the military that describes themselves as frogs. Jumping out of a helicopter to infiltrate a moving yacht wasn't exactly kosher. But it would have to do for now.

"I also have some toys in the back for you, if you want," he said playfully.

She glanced back at his clothing, but then, beneath it, she spotted a black duffel bag.

"Johnny paid for it," the pilot called out. "He must really like you.

That guy is stingy as all hell."

And now they were moving, cutting through the night sky, heading across the chain link fence below and circling the airfield.

As they moved, she reached into the backseat, snatched the duffel bag, and felt a bout of gratitude towards her ex-boyfriend. She didn't allow the emotion to last too long as she still remembered how things ended. Then again, maybe this was his way of making it up to her.

As she opened the bag, she nodded slowly.

"Night vision?"

"Check."

"Flash bang?"

"Also there."

"Is that a grappling hook?"

"Will help you secure to the rail of the boat. I tinkered with it a bit myself. Mechanism will be water resistant for a couple of hours at least."

"An M-16?"

"Set to burst fire. You can change it if you want, though." The pilot nodded a few times, his bonnet shifting up and down. "I should add there's a few extra magazines. The water will mess with the gear. So, the bag is lightweight and fully waterproof. You just have to zip it up, and then use that plastic seal on the end, see it there?"

Cora nodded and pressed.

"Well, thanks. How long until we reach the coordinates?"

"I'll plug them in once we get out over the water. Right now, flight control thinks I'm heading to Florida to pick up produce."

Cora nodded. She tensed, shifting uncomfortably.

She wondered what sort of hell Caitlin Johnson had been going through for the last two months.

With a horrible realization, Cora thought that, most likely, Caitlin didn't know what had happened to her mother.

At this thought, all she felt was a rising sense of sheer rage.

The thumping of the helicopter blades accompanied the pounding of her heart. Her hand tensed on the bag of gear, and she waited, quiet, staring through the windshield at the terrain below. The houses looked small. The lights dull.

Sometimes, the dark was just too much. It swallowed everything that seamed bright.

Then again, Cora had never seen an explosion that couldn't light up the horizon.

110

CHAPTER SEVENTEEN

Cora watched dark clouds blot out the moon.

Pitchforks of lightning cut through the sky. Below them, the ocean roiled, the waves splashing against the body of water where curling white met briny blue.

Cora stared through the windshield, shivering.

Even the lackadaisical pilot was shifting nervously at the controls.

The storm had been developing. Already, they had been flying for hours.

A small, red blip on a GPS system built into the dash was chirping now.

"I'm not sure how close I want to get to that storm," he said, uneasily.

The skies rumbled, rattling the glass from the thunder. Cora shifted uncomfortably, nodding as she did. "Anyway to get closer?" She paused, peering through the windshield. "If you can get me in front of the yacht, along its trajectory, I can take it from there."

A risky proposition, especially if the yacht was moving quickly and she missed her first grapple.

Then again, she trusted herself in the water; she had once spent three days on the open ocean.

She shot a look towards the half-naked pilot. "Just," she said hesitantly, "if you don't hear from me by tomorrow, come back on a pass. I'll use the glass from the night vision to reflect the sun."

He nodded, gripping the controls of the helicopter with tight hands.

Then, he seemed to reach a decision and veered forward, moving towards the storm.

The lightning continued to skewer the horizon. The roar of thunder continued to rattle the windows. Anyone besides a man like this, who Johnny had often bragged about based on his sheer recklessness, might have turned the helicopter around. But already, Cora knew she was running out of time.

Women didn't make it long in the trafficking world, especially if they were taken overseas.

Suddenly, as the lightning erupted, the beeping on the GPS grew louder. The red dot had a small circle flickering around it. She stared, peered through the glass and said, "There! I see it, down there! Is that it?"

"Looks right. Johnny is live tracking it based on radio communication."

"Okay, just get me ahead of it. Give me a few hundred yards."

He flashed a thumbs up, and pushed the controls forward, flying in lower. The one benefit of the storm, she decided, was that it would hide her approach.

As he accelerated, and they came in low, her heart pounded.

"You're sure this thing is waterproof?" She said, if only to say something and relieve some of her rising nerves. It had been a few years since she had done a water dive late at night, especially without teammates around.

The yacht was moving slowly through the storm, taking care against the waves. The snail pace of the thing would be at least some help.

"All right," the pilot said. "Get ready! I'm going to pass from North to South, directly. It will give them the smallest chance to spot us. I'm guessing you want to go in nosy, not noisy."

She nodded now, biting her lip, and tensed. She reached to her belt and unbuckled it. She hefted the supplies she'd been provided. Her phone, wallet, and everything of value has also been slipped inside the waterproof bag.

She would have to remember, grudgingly, to thank Johnny.

Cora said quickly, "Think the lightning will be enough for me to spot the yacht from the water?"

"I can drop a flare on it if you want. But they'll know I'm here."

Cora shook her head. "No, that's fine. I don't want to risk being seen. Let's go. This handle, right here?"

He nodded quickly. "I'm sure you know, but push away. I'll be giving you some distance as well. Just make sure to push away."

She nodded. She was no longer listening but watching with an unwavering gaze through the window, staring at the waters below.

The helicopter was picking up the pace, moving hastily forward, dropping lower now.

She was drawing near. Nearer still. And then they passed over the trajectory the yacht was on. She didn't have to wait to hear him shout, "Now!"

112

She twisted the lever, pushing the door. She inhaled deeply, hyperventilating to fill her lungs with a last, deep breath. With a desperate shout, she jumped out the door, waterproof bag strapped tightly to her arm. As she tumbled, her heart skipped, her skin was prickly, and her body was met by the cold, churning sea breeze. And she cut like an arrow, having thrown herself bodily from a moving helicopter into the path of an oncoming yacht. She made a point with her legs. The smallest amount of surface area possible to hit the smallest amount of surface area.

She cut through the water, slicing into the dark, roiling murk.

Salt in her mouth. Eyes. Everything wet. The sound of the splash swallowed by thunder, then cushioned by complete silence.

Cora managed to hold her breath and moved towards the surface, using the tickle of bubbles spilling up past her from air pockets in her clothing and her shoes to reorient. She thrashed back towards the surface.

The rolling water caught her, lifting her. As she elevated, she glimpsed the yacht, illuminated by another flash of lightning. Only a couple of hundred yards away, heading towards her.

She tensed and lifted the waterproof bag above her head. Doing her best to keep it fully removed from the liquid, she unzipped the corner, slipped a hand in, and withdrew the grappling launcher that she had stowed nearest the opening before jumping.

Removing this, she sealed the bag again and kept her eyes directed towards where she had seen the yacht. Without the lightning to illuminate, though, she lost sight of the oncoming boat. The thunder continued to rumble. The splash and the crash of water also served to disguise the sound of the boat, as well as that of the helicopter.

At least there was that. If she was having difficulty spotting the yacht, then she supposed they would have difficulty seeing the helicopter.

She managed to draw in a breath, deeply, calming herself, kicking to stay above the water.

It dipped once more, then lifted again. At least here, the waves weren't breaking.

She watched the horizon, resisting the urge to pull the night vision from inside the bag. These, she knew, would not survive the water.

As her body was carried up once more, she tensed and aimed.

The yacht was a hundred yards away.

She mimed the motion. Waiting. Thunder rumbling, another surge of the water. Another flash.

The boat was almost on her.

She began to kick, pushing herself out of the way of the prow. The goal was not to be slammed into by thousands of tons of steel, but to come alongside.

She would only have one shot if she waited too long; so, having moved out from the direct path of the oncoming yacht, she aimed, waited, watched as lightning flashed, glimpsed the spark of railing, and fired. Spluttering, water splashing, her hair soaked to her head, she cursed as the grappling hook fell too short.

Quickly, she began to reel it back in.

At the same time, she took heavy strokes in the water towards the oncoming boat.

The reason she had taken a preliminary shot was so that she could have a chance at a second one.

But if she missed this second time, there would be no doing it again. She reeled the hook, slid it into place, and aimed again.

This time, she couldn't wait for lightning.

She tracked the yacht based on the memory of its trajectory. Ahead, it was as if a shadow had been painted on another shadow. The hull was blocking out any attempts at ambient light.

She aimed a bit higher, fired. Then she gripped the rubber guard of the grappling launcher and waited.

It tugged. Slipped, the rope going slack, then went taut again.

She had hooked something.

She held on tight, skimming across the water as the yacht began to carry her like a fish on a hook.

And then, with painstaking motions, she wound the rope and pulled herself forward. Wound it again, pulled forward again. One foot at a time, she drew herself closer to the prize.

She was careful not to get too close as the water dropped. The wave would lift her again and might easily bring her skull crashing into the side.

She waited, and as the water dipped, and then rose again, she moved forward, quicker.

She bumped against the cold hull.

Portions of rust scraped against her arm.

She winced, teeth set tight.

And then kicking out, finding her balance, and winding the grappling hook some more, she began to climb the side of the boat, one

114

foot in front of the other: cautious, careful, and ascending with slow, sure-footed motions.

She walked up the side of the yacht, using the taut rope, water pouring off her in sheets, until she reached the rail.

The storm continued around her; if anything, it seemed to be getting more violent. She could feel the waves rising by the way her stomach lifted and fell.

She held onto the grappling tool and slipped over the railing, back scraping against frigid metal.

She unhooked the tool from where it had lodged against the rail, winced as she tensed and tested one of the prongs. Half bent, squished from the motion and her exertion.

But it had served its purpose.

She dropped the tool to the ground and dropped her duffel bag as well.

She fell to a knee, splattering water across the walkway and then, drying her hands as best as she could on the waterproof bag, she opened it, and began to remove items one at a time. The night vision goggles came first. She adjusted these but left them next to the bag for the moment.

The M-16 rifle, set to burst-fire, came next. She gripped it, her hands shaking from the cold. But as she held the familiar weapon, she found that she was able.

And then, slipping the flash bang grenade and the rest of her items into her sodden pockets, she lifted her gaze, scanning along the rails.

Painted in large, green letters on the side of the boat, she read, *Merchant.*

She scowled and shook her head, scattering more droplets of water; she supposed subtlety wasn't this man's strong suit. Instead of amusing, though, the bold lettering only increased her anger.

This man, like the one back at the warehouse, traded in souls. He didn't just capture them but submitted them to torment.

Caitlin Johnson was under the mercy of the Merchant.

But this boat, at least for now, was at *Cora's* mercy.

Her vision was consumed by green light. The occasional flash of lightning illuminated the headwear, temporarily blinding her. But as the light vanished, her sight returned.

She moved along the wet walkway, her weapon clutched tight, taking one step in front of the other.

Two men were walking up metal stairs, moving quickly, arms

braced on the rails. One of them had an AK-47 strapped to his chest. The other had a submachine gun hooked over his shoulder.

The M-16 had come with a silencer; she had toggled the firing mode from burst to single shot.

She was waiting for the thunder.

The two men, gripping their illegal firearms, didn't see a thing.

Suddenly, lightning flashed.

One of the men froze, and she realized he was staring directly at her.

She stood, her feet shoulder width apart, as water speckled the ground.

She waited a second, even though the man had seen her. His gun began to raise, and she heard a faint shout.

And then the thunder roared.

And she squeezed the trigger twice.

Two shots: one to the chest and one to the head.

She moved in the same motion and got off two more shots before the thunder faded again.

The next flash of lightning, as rain pelted the side of the ship, illuminated two corpses on the metal stairs.

She hastened forward, pausing next to the man with the AK-47. She fished in his pockets, pulling out a set of keys and a magnetic strip ID card. He had money, which she didn't recognize, and a roll of mints. The mints she tossed aside but the key card and the keys she slipped into her own pocket.

And then, she kept moving.

Occasionally, she thought she heard voices. But it was difficult to make out in the storm. This particular yacht had three levels.

She was currently on the second.

She paused, leaning her back against the rail, feeling the water prickle her face as raindrops continued to fall.

Then, twisting, she arched over the rail, peering up and then down.

She spotted another figure, his hand on the rail below her, moving slowly.

But above her, through the rail, she spotted four men. Two of them were shivering, leaning against the metal support in the storm. She guessed that they didn't particularly want to be out in this, but they had drawn the short straw. Two more men were moving hastily, footsteps clapping against the metal.

She heard one of them saying, "Boss wants more wine. Fat bastard can choke on it for all I care."

Another voice replied, "Better keep that to yourself. Unless you want him to feed you to his fish."

Cora decided the third level was where the action was at.

She moved towards the stairs at the end of the metal walkway, taking them two at a time. And then, movements at the top of the stairs. Perhaps the men who had been sent to fetch more beverages.

One of them had a weapon on his shoulder. The other, though, wore a white uniform.

She didn't hesitate. Two bullets into the man with the gun. He fell. She pointed her weapon at the second man, held a finger to her lips, and then beckoned with her hand for him to approach.

He stared at her, stunned, as the man she had shot slipped down the stairs on his chest, lifeless.

She beckoned more insistently, now scowling.

Reluctantly, hands raised, a look of terror on his face, the man in the white uniform approached.

She kept her gun pointed at him, watching the green figure through her night vision goggles.

"The Merchant," she hissed, venom in her voice. "Where is he?"

The man pointed over his shoulder with a trembling finger. "Upstairs. He's on a business call!"

She nodded, then brought her gun hard into his chin.

He hit the deck like a sack of wet potatoes.

But she was moving, stepping over the fallen form, past the man she had shot, kicking his gun down the stairs.

She exhaled slowly, standing in the rain, feeling the rocking of the boat on the water.

There would be two more men at the top of the stairs. The ones she had seen against the rail.

She waited, counting and watching for lightning, and then emerged.

The lightning illuminated the men. Both of them were armed, one of them spotted her.

He just blinked, quizzically.

And that was all he managed.

The thunder came next. And so did the gunshots.

Four bullets.

Two bodies.

And she kept moving.

CHAPTER EIGHTEEN

She hastened across the slick deck, moving over the two corpses.

There was a large, ornate door made of glass and a white frame set in the side of the third deck.

A bright, orange glow illuminated from inside this space.

Cora peered through the glowing window, her back pressed to the metal hull. Within, she was confronted by an unusual sight. Then again, most of this yacht was unusual. She didn't make a habit of frequenting luxury vessels. But through the glass, she spotted figures lounging in a pool.

Two women. One of them was sitting on some submerged steps, nursing a bruised cheek. Her nose was bleeding and trickling into the water. Steam rose around them from vents. A second woman was handing a white towel to the bleeding woman, comforting her, one hand on her shoulder. Both of them were shooting furtive glances towards an open door in the back of the room, from which the steam was emanating.

The window was large, encapsulating most of the wall to provide those in the pool with a view of the ocean, no doubt. Plus, despite the storm, swimming in a pool under cover wasn't as dangerous as swimming beneath a sky filled with lightning.

Still, the two women in the pool seemed to have other concerns.

The water in the pool itself was sloshing, shifting back and forth with the rising and falling of the boat on the storming waves. But the steam itself, trapped behind the glass, was like a declaration of indifference. The women inside didn't seem to notice. One of them paused to adjust a bathing suit, lowering the towel she had used to dab the blood from the other.

Cora watched, feeling a rising sense of anger as another figure emerged from the steam. The man wore a cotton, white bathrobe and a giant, shit-eating grin above a wobbly double-chin.

Cora pressed her hand against the glass, reaching for the handle but as she tried to turn it, her fingers slipped on rain-speckled metal. The door handle wouldn't budge.

She frowned, still peering through the glass. The large man in the white bathrobe was now beckoning towards the two women. He was raising his voice, yelling at them. The two women in the swimming pool quailed under the deluge of his verbal assault.

Cora pressed her teeth tightly together.

She watched the glass as the large man waved a hand about, gesticulating wildly. He had diamond rings on his fingers. And, nestled in his hirsute chest, a golden pendant dangled.

The man continued to raise his voice, waving a hand around and shouting.

Cora glanced once more at the lock and spotted a small magnetic strip. She yanked the key card she had found on the dead guard out of her pocket and flashed it across the keypad.

A blinking of green light. A quiet *click*, barely audible over the drumming rain. Then, she turned the handle and pushed the door, which opened instantly.

She shouldered into the room, her weapon in hand.

She caught the final words of the large man's tirade. "You nearly cost me that call, you little whore!" he was screaming. He pointed a finger at the woman with the bloodied nose. "You're lucky that's all you got!"

Cora didn't recognize either of the swimmers. Caitlin wasn't here. But it was a large ship, and the man who could point her in the right direction was currently standing across the pool, displaying far more skin than she was comfortable with.

"Stop where you are!" she barked.

The man with the many jeweled rings rounded sharply, staring at her, wide-eyed.

She gestured with her gun, waving him to stand away from the women.

The two women had frozen in the pool, stunned. Their expressions were equal parts frightened and verging on hopeful.

Clearly, though, life had dealt them such a hand that they weren't confident whether this was a rescue or an execution.

Cora braced her gun, aiming at the corpulent aggressor.

Instead of stepping aside, though, his eyes narrowed in a mean, piggy face. He snarled and surged forward, moving clumsily, his bare feet slapping against the tiled ground. He snatched at the woman with the bloodied nose and dragged her to her feet. At the same time, he flung his robe aside, giving another glimpse that Cora wished she could unsee. But also revealing a knife strapped to his ample waist. This emerged in his hand, while his other squeezed at the neck of the woman staring across the pool.

He pressed the knife to her throat, glaring over her damp hair.

The woman was frozen in terror. Her friend in the pool was scrambling back, trying to get out, panic in every desperate motion. Cora felt the boat rock again, the lightning flashing behind her cast her silhouette across the sloshing pool. The thick steam twirled, assuaging her cheeks and spreading through the space.

The weapon in her hand remained steady; the man with the knife pressed to the woman's neck stared at her, blinking a few times as sweat dripped down his face. He said, "I don't believe I know you."

He had no accent, his dark eyebrows and bristling black hair were the only hints at his Mediterranean heritage. He gripped the knife tight, the curved end digging into the woman's chin.

"American government?" He asked.

She shook her head and said, "Let her go or I'm going to kill you."

But the man only hunched, ducking behind the woman, using her as a shield. The other woman was still moving back, trying to keep distant.

Cora stood frozen to the spot. "Are you the man known as the Merchant?"

He didn't deny it but also didn't affirm it. Instead, he said slowly, "And who is asking?"

She looked him dead in the eyes. "I'm the one that's going to shoot you if you don't let that woman go."

Another growl of thunder. More flashing lightning. Cora shifted uncomfortably, wincing as she did.

There was no clear shot. The large man was bowed behind his victim. The woman with the blood streaming from her nose was still hyperventilating, the skin on her neck pressing harder against the knife. A slow trickle of blood fell down her throat.

Cora was shivering now. The wind coming through the open door behind her speckled her shoulders and arms with more droplets of freezing rain. She was still dripping, standing in a puddle she had caused.

"Where is Caitlin Johnson?" Cora snapped.

The moment she said the name, two reactions caught her attention. The second woman who had been tending to the victim's bloodied nose glanced over, sharply. The man with the knife, though, didn't seem to register the name at all. Instead, he wrinkled his nose in contempt and growled at her, "Lower that gun, or I slit her throat!"

Cora felt another jolt of rage. But also, he looked as if he was serious.

Amidst the room full of swirling steam, on either ends of a pool on the third level of a luxury yacht, the tension raged.

Cora didn't lower her weapon, and she didn't blink.

The man with the knife glared back. The two of them held each other's gaze, until at last, the large man snarled and spat, "Fine!"

And then with a heavy shove, he sent the woman stumbling forward. At the same time, he used the momentum to push off her, racing back through the door he had used earlier, stepping into a cloud of billowing steam.

CHAPTER NINETEEN

Cora rushed forward, feet hitting wet tile as she nearly slipped. She caught her balance, arms waving, hastening past the woman struggling in the water.

Cora took one second to drop to a knee, grab the woman's wrist, and pull her back onto the tile.

As she did, the other woman, on the opposite side of the pool, met Cora's gaze. She still had that strange look of recognition.

Cora shot a look towards the steaming room, but then glanced back at the woman. "Do you know Caitlin Johnson?" she insisted.

The woman swallowed, shooting a nervous look towards the steam. But then, rapidly, in a whisper, her eyes fixed where Cora was helping her friend out of the pool, she rattled off, "The name sounds familiar. The new girls go to a compound, though."

"Compound, where?"

"Umm...I...Please..."

"Tell me where!" Cora insisted. "You're safe. I promise."

The woman swallowed, then continued, "It's on a small island near Columbia. The jurisdiction is shaky. That's why he likes it." She had an educated, articulate way of speaking.

Cora was pushing back to her feet, gun pointed towards the steamy room. "Does the compound have a name?"

The woman continued at a rapid pace, "They call it the Silver Bracelet. Once a woman comes through there, they're trained..." She trailed off, a look of shame and rage in her eyes, "And then sent to international clients. United Arab Emirates or places in Mexico. If I remember right, the next shipment is heading out in two days."

Cora was breathing heavily, nodding as she did. A few days? Had Caitlin already been shipped off, lost in the world? Or was there still a chance? Two days wasn't long, not at all.

She gave a quick nod of gratitude towards the woman, pointed at the injured lady, and whispered, "Take care of her." Then, Cora hastened away from the fallen woman as her new source of information hurried around the pool to help.

Cora approached the steam-filled room. She had her gun in front of her, her heart pounding.

She stepped into the room and was assailed by the murky atmosphere. She couldn't see more than a couple of feet in front of her.

She crouched, keeping her head low, just in case more than a knife was waiting for her in this sauna.

The ground was now made of black tile. Her feet thumped against the floor.

It was as if the steam itself had a muffling effect; she could no longer hear the woman behind her. But she also didn't detect any sound from within this new room.

Cora tried to trace the layout and was able to make out marble benches carved into the wall.

Her feet continued to slap against the slick floor. She thought she saw movement and fired; she heard a loud hiss. And then a sudden sound of a slamming door.

She bolted towards the noise.

There had been another door in the back of the room. As she pushed through, she suddenly darted back, a knife swiping at her face.

She dodged, slamming the door again, and braced behind the door, tense. She waited a second and then tried again.

This time, as she pushed through the second door, she found her fingers pressing glass and a sudden cold chill of rainwater as she emerged at another set of metal stairs.

She heard the thumping of footsteps against the stairs. A sudden, loud voice. "Stop her! Shoot her!"

She tried to aim. Glimpsed a silhouette moving down the stairs. But as she sighted, two more figures emerged. One of them raised his gun.

She redirected her aim. Fired. Caught the man in the shoulder, sending him wheeling off the ship; he plummeted into the choppy sea.

But she had missed her opportunity to hit the Merchant. He was now out of sight on the second deck somewhere.

She pressed her teeth tightly together but had ducked back out of sight. Bullets rattled off the underside of the metal platform. The second man was more cautious than the first.

She waited, counting slowly before she broke into a sprint, taking the stairs three at a time. She repositioned on the next landing.

The man directly below her tried to fire through the floor. For one horrible moment, she wasn't sure if the metal would hold. It punctured, like gofer holes, but the bullets didn't hit her.

She pressed her gun against one of the holes and fired twice.

A sound of pain, and then a dull thump.

Cautiously, heart in her throat, she moved down the stairs.

Her mind was spinning. If the woman upstairs was correct, then Caitlin Johnson only had a couple of days until she was lost for good.

Where was that corpulent trafficker?

She hurried down the steps now, gun in front of her. Another soldier lay on the ground, dead.

And then, she heard a new sound. It wasn't the rumble of thunder, but more like the growl of an engine.

Her heart fell.

A boat was scything away from the large ship.

She blinked, stunned. A speedboat, sleek and white. A billowing bathrobe whipped the air behind the pilot. The boat skimmed off a rising wall of water and hit the other side with a calamitous splash.

She stared as the boat cut a white wake, hastening rapidly away.

He'd had an escape route. She felt a jolt of fury. Normally, she would have been far more knowledgeable about the options on a mission field, but she simply hadn't had time.

And now, the one man who could lead her directly to Caitlin was escaping.

CHAPTER TWENTY

Cora watched from over the railing, hidden in the shadows beneath the stairs in the dead of night. She'd been the one to make the distress call from the bridge's radio.

And now, an hour after the Merchant had escaped, she watched the fruit of her labor.

A fleet of coast guard boats hastened towards her, flying across the water. The flashing red lights from the boats illuminated the roiling ocean; the storm was coming now, and the lightning had vanished.

This aided her in staying on scene.

She waited until the boats came alongside the yacht. Ropes lashed to the side of the larger vessel. Men and women on bullhorns called out to each other.

Cora waited, tense, exhaling slowly.

She watched as members of the Coast Guard moved up the ladders on the side of the large vessel, swarming the ship.

Footsteps clamored against the stairwell above her head, serving as her shelter.

As the first wave moved past her, leaving her unseen in the shadows, she slowly emerged.

She slipped down the side of the boat, using the same cold metal rungs they had utilized to board the ship, and then she clambered down to one of the smaller vessels.

In that moment, no one spotted her; she heard shouting, radio chatter, and more footsteps as other members of the Coast Guard reached the opposite side of the ship. The bodies were no doubt being found.

She hit the deck of the smaller vessel, cut the rope, and, shivering, disengaged the GPS and onboard locating system.

Wires pricked at her fingers as she tugged them loose, and then gunned the engine; she began to dislodge from the main boat. A voice called over the radio, "Unit three—come in, unit three—where are you going?"

But she switched off the radio and pushed full throttle.

She cut away from the large vessel, slicing through the water and hastening out to sea.

With this done, she shot a look over her shoulder. The wind caught her hair, the spray from the ocean flecked her cheeks. No one was in pursuit.

She sped away, heart in her throat. Once she was sure that no one was giving chase, she unzipped the bag on her shoulder, withdrew her phone with numb fingers, and quickly placed a call. "Johnny, can you hear me?" She said, her voice shaking.

"Cora? I can't hear you."

She hunched a bit at the helm of the boat skimming over the waves. She shouted, louder, "Can you hear me now?"

"I can hear you. Did you find what you were looking for. Shit, there's all sorts of radio chatter where you're at."

Cora frowned. "If I didn't know better, I would have thought you were concerned for me."

He chuckled a bit. "Good to hear you're still kicking. Did you find him?"

"He got away," she said, her voice tinged with bitterness. She tasted salt and spat. She then said, "I need another favor." Before he could bellyache about this, she continued the ask, "There's a compound, near a small island off the coast of Columbia. It's called Silver Bracelet or something like that. Apparently, there's some sticky jurisdiction. I need the coordinates."

"All right, give me a second. I'm in the john, anyhow."

"Charming," she retorted.

She heard the sound of movement, silence, and then a few minutes passed. She continued over the water, speeding across the ocean with no sign of pursuit.

Then, Johnny spoke again. "Cora, you hear me?"

"Do I want to? Don't forget to wash your hands."

"Very funny. Look, you can't go there."

She was surprised by the severity of his tone. "What do you mean?"

"Which word are you struggling with? Maybe I can define it."

"Do you have the coordinates or not?"

"I mean it, Cora, you don't want to go to this place. It's bad news. I'm looking at some surveillance photos taken by the CIA, and from what I can tell, there's at least thirty armed men there. It's not so much a compound as a militia outpost. You should stay clear."

"No can do. Coordinates."

A heavy sigh. Then, more insistent, "Can't you send this along to someone? What about the FBI?"

"Not happening. The FBI isn't going to listen to me. I'm not exactly in their good graces. Look, I have to do this. You know as well as me, especially if there's jurisdictional gray areas, the American government isn't going to do anything about a few unlucky, lower-class women. Now, coordinates."

"Why are you so damn muleheaded?"

"Maybe it's contagious. I must have learned it from you. Now give me those coordinates, Johnny. I'm serious."

"And here I was, thinking you were joking. All right, I know what you're doing."

"What do you think I'm doing?"

"You know exactly what you're doing."

Cora wrinkled her nose. "Johnny, I'm not in the mood for word games. How about you just give me those coordinates, and I promise I'll stop bothering you."

He made a scoffing sound. "Right, because I'm just going to let you wander off into a compound of soldiers completely unprotected. That's totally going to happen."

Cora frowned. She couldn't quite understand the tone of his voice. He sounded equal parts angry and resigned. But resigned to what?

"Look, you're going to need to resupply anyway..." he trailed off. But then, speaking twice as quickly, if to simply get it out in the air, he said, "Why don't you meet me at the coordinates I sent? It's about thirty minutes away from the compound. But it will give us a chance to tactically assemble."

"What are you talking about?"

"Don't pretend that this wasn't your plan all along."

"What plan, Johnny?"

"Of course, I'm not going to let you go off into a militia compound without backup. What sort of frogman would I be? I want you to hear, for the record, that I've never had any trouble like this from the others."

"Johnny, I'm not asking you to help. Just send me the damn coordinates."

"Sending now. The location is nearby. We'll meet there. I'll bring some body armor, couple of grenades, and maybe some other toys we can use. I mean, Christ, Cora, what am I supposed to do here? Watch you die?"

Cora blinked, partially due to the spray from the ocean, but also in surprise. She hadn't realized Johnny cared. He was always making wisecracks, teasing, and mocking. Besides, the last time they had been together, it had ended like the Hindenburg. She wasn't sure what to make of his offer. In a way, she felt a faint lump in her throat. Standing there, on the boat, at the helm, she realized something. She hadn't taken any pills in a couple of days now. In fact, the adrenaline-laced evening had filled her with a sense of exhilaration that dwarfed the effect of the pills and the alcohol.

Being kicked out of the FBI had only confirmed her worst suspicions—she was alone in this world.

But maybe not as alone as she thought. She hadn't even asked for help. Perhaps, much to her shame. But there Johnny was, offering it regardless.

She said slowly, "You really don't have to."

"Cora, I mean this sincerely, just shut up. I'll meet you there. How far do you think you are?"

"Pretty far. And I'm on a dinky little boat. Full fuel, though. I'd say if I pilot through the night, I should get there sometime tomorrow afternoon. Just send me the coordinates."

And then she hung up, her spine tingling, adrenaline coursing through her system.

CHAPTER TWENTY ONE

Cora watched the blinking light on the map open on her phone. The scent of the ocean had now been replaced with the fragrance of diesel and fuel. The fumes lingered above the wooden docks. A couple of large, rusted ships sat on stilts, halfway up the shore. It was nearly two in the afternoon; now she had been on the move for more than twenty-four hours.

She wondered how many days she could go without a full night of sleep. As tough as her training had been, even a soldier had limits.

She moved with some haste to the side of the wooden dock, coming to a stop where the prow gouged into the splintered wood.

She was too tired to do it properly.

There was the sound of some dockworkers, merrily trading stories and shouting instructions that she couldn't understand.

A few of the men cast glances in her direction.

She ignored them, scanning the dock, looking for—

"Took you long enough," came the leonine voice of her old flame.

She glanced towards a small, wooden kiosk. A man was reading a newspaper clutched in his hand.

The man looked over and she met his gaze.

His hair was longer than she remembered: dark, curling and brushing past his eyes. He had stubble along his chin and a strong, masculine jaw.

He was handsome, though she didn't allow her mind to linger; his hands were calloused and where he was gripping the newspaper, she noted that the pinky finger on his right hand was missing.

He lowered the paper, stretched, and pulled himself to his full height. Six foot even, and he still had the trim physique of an athlete.

"Looking good," he said, nodding slowly and approaching her. There was a wolfish quality to his gaze. An almost predatory look in his eyes that she had always remembered—Johnny was not a safe man. He wasn't a particularly kind man. But he was loyal and deadly.

It was part of what had made their time together fun. Though she wouldn't tell him, part of what was giving her some small sense of gratitude was that he had agreed to come with her. Knowing that he would be at her side was a comfort in and of itself.

He reached into the wooden kiosk and pulled out a larger duffel bag, seemingly made of the same fabric as the one she had.

"Toys?" He asked, raising an eyebrow. He added, "Hohoho."

"All right, Santa," she murmured. "Let's see what you have." Cora watched as he removed the body armor first, handing it to her.

She shot a look at the dockworkers and quirked an eyebrow. He said, "Don't worry about them. They're friends."

Cora took the armor. As she began to tug at her shirt to place the armor on beneath the outer layer, she paused and frowned. "Why are you doing this?"

There was a momentary silence. Even the dockworkers had gone quiet, though Cora could still hear the noise of the water lapping against the dock

Johnny studied her and shook his head. "Why not?"

"No, really. Don't be cute. Why?"

"First, you want me to take you out. Next, you think I'm cute. But for real, I'm not letting you go in alone." Those wolfish eyes studied her, and he flashed a grin that was closer to a leer, showing teeth.

She said, "It's not going to be pretty. There is no shame in backing out."

"This is about Adder's kid, right?"

"That's right."

"What they do to one of us, they do to all of us. Now shut up and put it on. I've got some more toys here. And then we should probably get going."

Cora was nodding. She said, "According to the woman back on that yacht, we have about another day until the girls at the compound are shipped out overseas. If that happens," she shook her head, "I'm not sure if we will ever see them again."

And so, with quick motions, Cora pulled off her outer layer and put on the bulletproof vest. Then, returning her shirt, she accepted a new clip of ammunition and a tactical belt from which dangled two grenades. She took the flash bang from her own bag, attaching it to the belt; the two of them worked in grim silence, handing items and withdrawing as if they had been practicing the motions.

They had gone on more than one mission together in the past. And in a way, the scent of saltwater on the air, it felt like the old days.

This time, though, she wondered if they would make it out alive.

She shivered at the thought. What if Johnny was shot? What if she failed Caitlin?

Then again, questions like that didn't have good answers.

No, it was far better to focus on the positive.

In, out. The two of them against an army.

Things would have to go their way, but at least they had the element of surprise. Two of them trained, SEALs with significant combat experience.

They couldn't afford to take the enemy lightly, though.

Their lives depended on it. Caitlin Johnson's life, and her entire future, depended on it.

CHAPTER TWENTY TWO

Caitlin stood trembling, her arms prickling, goosebumps along her back. She wore a red dress cut at the knee. She could still smell the soap in her hair, where she had been told to clean and prepare.

This was a far more comfortable outfit and atmosphere than her sprint through the jungle; now, she wore shoes, makeup, and perfume.

Now, she had a belly satiated with food.

And yet her current horror was far greater than what she had experienced back in the jungle, fleeing armed men.

She stood in front of a room full of men.

Older men with leering faces. Many of them dressed ostentatiously. The scent of alcohol lingered heavily on the air. Other women, also wearing red dresses, moved through the room, carrying drinks to various clients.

The men all sat in a sort of theater arrangement.

Caitlin stood on a wooden stage, shifting uncomfortably, watching one of the soldiers who had dragged her from the jungle.

This man, with a thick beard and one pale eye, was addressing the others in the room, speaking a language she didn't understand.

He had a small little gavel in one hand that he tapped against the counter every time he wanted their attention.

And now, in the spacious room, standing on the stage, feeling more terror than she ever had, she watched as the men raised brochures, or cups, responding to comments made by the bearded soldier.

In the back of the room, Caitlin had watched as a large man with a double chin and wearing many jeweled rings on his fingers had appeared.

He was wearing a crimson suit, matching the color of the dresses that the women had been forced to wear.

The man in the suit was nodding, reading various figures. More than thirty of the patrons, who had been responding to what she could only describe as an auction, had sat up, some had even regained their feet, and nodded in deference towards this newcomer.

The man in the crimson suit with the jeweled rings moved to a

132

place of honor at the largest seat in the center of the table.

He smiled at a few of the girls serving drinks, gesturing for them to bring him new refreshments.

Something about the look in his small eyes made her skin crawl; she had considered making a run for it. But this, she had eventually decided, would be a mistake.

There were too many men. Soldiers with guns posted at the various doors that led out of the room. She was trapped.

And the men were still bidding on her.

The man with the beard gestured at her, frowning. "Sing," he said in English.

She blinked in surprise.

He waved at her, and snapped, "Dance, sing!"

She swallowed slowly, feeling a flush of embarrassment.

Most of the patrons were laughing, watching her.

She could sense their arousal at her humiliation. Could sense the lecherous, predatory look in their demonic eyes.

"Sing now!" snapped the bearded man.

She hesitated, preparing to refuse. And just then, there was a sound of a loud explosion.

For a moment, everyone's attention was diverted.

Caitlin wrinkled her nose, glancing off.

A few of the soldiers by the doors were pressing fingers to their ears, chattering into their radios.

The large man in the crimson suit got to his feet now, wearing a look of horror. He was rattling off instructions to another man who was sitting next to him, carrying an AK-47.

And then, there was the sound of a second explosion.

Caitlin tensed, watching wide-eyed. Some of the other women in the room shared panicked looks.

But their fright was nothing compared to the looks of terror on the faces of the patrons. Many of the wealthy, luxuriously dressed men tried to get to their feet, to start moving towards the exit, but the man in the crimson suit started shouting, waving his hands and ushering for them to remain seated.

Soldiers were now filing towards the exits, weapons at the ready.

The explosions were getting closer. And then, in the distance, Caitlin heard gunfire.

This did not elicit the same terror from her that she could see in the faces around her. Rather, she found herself reacting with a surge of hope.

Anything was better than what she was standing in. Any outcome was a definite improvement.

The gunfire was getting closer, the explosions still ringing in her ears. The mutters of terror now lingering in the room, from the men who had been drinking and bidding on her as if she were a slab of meat, was music to her ears.

CHAPTER TWENTY THREE

Cora hadn't *meant* to blow up the ship. The grenade, however, had hit a fuel tank.

And then, all hell had broken loose.

Johnny and Cora sat low in the stolen Coast Guard vessel, braced against the edge of the ship, as a salvo of bullets carved through the deck.

Smoke and flames billowed in the air, coming from the boat that they had hit with the grenade.

It had cost them the element of surprise. But five soldiers had been gathered on the boat—too good of an opportunity to pass up.

Johnny now sat up, fired twice, and ducked again.

He looked at her, eyes wide, grin even wider. "Two more," he muttered.

He looked ecstatic, and his face was streaked with dark paint of browns and mottled green, intended to help blend in with the small island's flora.

They hadn't had time to wait for the evening.

Cora had made the call to start their assault under the sunlight.

They needed to find Caitlin, and they needed to move quickly.

Their boat glided to shore, scraping the hull as it bit into the sand.

The sudden cessation of the forward momentum sent the two of them stumbling. More bullets whipped through the air. Splinters of wood geysered off the rail.

Quiet *tinging* sounds accompanied gunfire.

Cora waited for a brief lull, then emerged. She glimpsed three men off to the left, standing by a shipping container that had been taken to shore. Three more men were sprinting from the direction of low buildings that looked like barracks. Others could be glimpsed, smaller, moving towards them.

She aimed towards the men by the shipping container and squeezed twice.

Burst fire.

The men hit the ground, their guns going suddenly quiet.

But now, the cover of their boat was nearly completely destroyed.

"Johnny, move fast. Ready?"

He glanced at her hand, which was gripping the flash bang, and he nodded once, his eyes flashing.

She tensed, pulled the pin, and then flung the concussion grenade through the air in the direction of the largest clump of soldiers she had spotted earlier.

She remained ducked for a few seconds, then heard a loud *clap!*

"Now!" she yelled. The two of them vaulted the badly damaged railing, over the side of the sinking boat, whose perforation had failed to keep it afloat.

The front of the boat still gouged in the sand, turning it up like wet pastry.

For a brief moment, there was a lull in the gunfire, thanks to the grenade, as the two of them raced forward.

Smoke billowed in her face, and Cora vaulted one of the bodies. The black plumes and red jets sprang in bounding flickers from the burning ship. She heard shouting in the distance now. The chatter of weapons.

She flung herself to the ground, pushing Johnny. The two of them ate sand, hitting the sandy shore hard. But even as clumps of wet sand spewed with the insistence of bullets, she aimed and fired.

Another soldier down. Johnny, meanwhile, was pulling one of the grenades. He launched.

A pause. Something hot lanced across her arm.

Then a *boom!*

A tree toppled and three men went flying, their shouts of warning cut short.

Cora and Johnny bolted forward, breaking to the trees, pausing to take their shots, then moving onto the next trunk for cover.

More men were streaming from the compound.

Johnny and Cora, both breathing heavily, stood with their backs to a large trunk. Sweat poured down Cora's face. Johnny was still grinning, his face streaked with ash from where the smoke had lingered.

"Ready?" he hissed at her, unhooking a smoke from his belt.

She frowned at him.

He gave a quick shake. "Both of us can't move. They'll pin us against the compound wall. I'll keep 'em here. You move."

Cora frowned. "I'm not splitting up."

"That's not what you said three years ago."

She tried to retort, but a sudden burst of gunfire cut her short. Wood and bark erupted in splinters from the tree.

She hissed, "Now's not the time for wisecracks."

But he had already pulled the pin, hefted the smoke grenade, aimed, and tossed it. A sudden hiss accompanied the arching incendiary. Smoke billowed in gray plumes, mingling with the black streaks arising from the burning hull in the dock.

More shouting. A few more bursts of gunfire. But then, as the smoke spread, the shooting faded. Voices called out to one another. Figures moved through the smoke, tentatively. One, disoriented, came too close.

Johnny put him down with a double tap to the head.

"Go," he whispered to her, giving a little nudge in the small of her back. "They're peeling off west. Take the eastern wall. Find this girl of yours."

Cora exhaled shakily. She didn't like the idea of leaving a team member alone. But Johnny knew how to take care of himself.

Caitlin on the other hand...

Cora reached a decision, patted him on the shoulder once, then broke into a sprint, racing through the trees without firing—she didn't want them to track her through the smoke.

She cut through the smoke, keeping low, trying to step lightly. Now, the shouting faded off over her shoulder. She was able to tell the direction of the approaching gunmen.

Johnny kept shooting. Shouting as well, drawing as much attention to himself as possible. The smoke was now spreading between them, like tendrils of lingering vapor.

She lost sight of her companion, and then pushed on, breathing heavily as she raced towards the compound. She spotted the fence soon enough as the smoke's lingering effects began to recede the more she distanced herself from it.

A single guard was sitting in a guardhouse, peering down the barrel of his rifle, eye to a scope. She approached cautiously, moving hurriedly.

The man aimed and exhaled, depleting his lungs.

She flung her knife.

It buried into his throat and the guard toppled from his overlook, hitting the ground with a dull *thump*.

She scrambled up the fence now, climbed into the guardhouse and dropped down the other side. Breathing rapidly, fingers tingling from

137

the effort of exertion, she scanned the compound. Two main buildings were visible from her vantage point.

One—a squat, gray thing—was likely a barracks judging by the way the door had been left haphazardly open, allowing a glimpse of a toppled table and scattered playing cards.

Beyond it, though, she spotted a larger structure, painted green, as if at least some effort had been made to pretty up the place.

"Bingo," she murmured. As far as mantras went, not a particularly meaningful one, but it helped propel her feet forward all the same, and she raced towards the structure.

She approached the doors, moving cautiously. The sound of gunfire continued behind her.

As long as it continued, it meant that Johnny was still stirring the hornet's nest, giving her a chance to execute the mission.

She didn't approach the door, but rather went to a window, pressing her face to the glass.

Inside the room, through the smudged window, she spotted men taking shelter below tables. She spotted a figure on a wooden stage, swaying with the sound of gunfire as if responding to some music. She couldn't make out much in the way of features, though. Her own breath fogged the glass.

She slid along the wall, scraping her back as she approached the door now.

She exhaled slowly, pausing, rehearsing what she'd seen through the window.

One guard standing in front of the door. The other off to the left, waiting. Guns in hand.

She hesitated, aimed her own weapon from memory, pointing it at the wooden door, then fired twice.

The bullets punctured the wood. A pause.

Then a thump of a body hitting the floor.

She didn't hesitate now, though, but kicked out *hard*. The door shattered, flinging open, the wooden frame slamming into the second man who'd been hiding behind the door.

She stepped in.

Two more bullets.

He hit the ground.

Instantly, surveying the room, she spotted another soldier at a back door. He managed to shoot. A bullet whizzed past her cheek.

She fired back.

He lost his cheek.

She stepped into the room now, over the new corpses, shouting, "On the ground! Everyone on the ground. I will blow you away if—"

One of the figures was moving, hand darting towards a weapon.

She shot him dead.

Another man was slinking off towards an exit door. She shot him in the leg.

"Stay down!" She yelled. "Down, now!"

Slowly, the twenty or so figures hiding beneath the tables raised their hands, going flat on their bellies.

And only then did her eyes land on the woman standing on the stage.

Smoke continued to billow through the door behind her, curling at her ankles. Gunfire peppered the skyline. Blood lapped against her combat boots. Her fingers were sore from the heavy work of merciless execution.

But there, in a red dress, her eyes landed on a sight that assuaged her sore eyes.

She swallowed, reached up and rubbed an eye, then blinked. The smoke must have stung her eyeballs. She found that they were watering, stinging.

She cleared her throat, voice shaking. "You—you look just like her."

The young woman in the red dress had the same golden hair, pulled back. The same high cheekbones and upturned nose. Just like her aunt.

Like her mother.

Caitlin Johnson stared back at her.

"Do I know you?" she said, the young woman's voice trembling horribly. She stared wide-eyed across the room. Occasionally, she shot glances at the men hiding beneath the benches, then at the men Cora had shot.

"Come on," Cora said sharply. "I'm a friend of your mother's. Let's go, Caitlin!"

The woman hesitated only a moment, swallowing. She adjusted the strap on her red dress, shaking. Instead of leaping off the stage or shooting suspicious looks at Cora, Caitlin said, "There are others. We have to help them too."

"We will!" Cora snapped.

Already, her phone was out, placing the call. They'd discussed this en route. She was intent on notifying Agent Brady. He'd handle it from

139

there. She had to call him late enough that Johnny and Cora could get away without incident or detention.

But soon enough that the rest of the men on the island couldn't flee.

Then again, where would they flee too? Their boat was blown to bits.

Cora gestured more urgently at Caitlin. "We have it handled. Help will come for them. You need to come with me, *now*!"

The gunfire had faded behind her. With it, her heart increased in tempo. She nodded once, confirming her decision to herself. Brady would handle it. Brady would have contacts with foreign authorities. The deputy would get involved.

And Cora...

She'd put it all in her rearview mirror.

She gestured once more at Caitlin. But the girl was still hesitant, glancing back over her shoulder. Cora said, firmly, "They're going to be fine. There isn't room for them now. Come!"

And then, at this first sentence, Caitlin finally hastened down from the stage and rushed towards Cora, her dress smoothed in front of her as she pressed with her hands, conserving modesty. But after a few steps, the sounds of battle faded. An eerie silence approached, interspliced by mewls from the man who was shot in the leg, as Caitlin abandoned decorum and broke into a sprint, following Cora's rapid gestures.

Cora kept her gun trained on the men on the ground. She moved with Caitlin, hastening back through the door. Every so often she shot glances at the young woman, making sure that she was still there.

She stepped backwards, out into the compound.

The only warning came in the form of Caitlin's scream.

The door slammed shut, sealing Cora back in the compound. As she whirled, something struck her *hard* across the back of the head.

CHAPTER TWENTY FOUR

Cora blinked blearily, head spinning. As her eyes adjusted, she froze.

The Merchant was standing with his gun pressed to Caitlin's head. He sneered down at her, his jowls wobbling, his many ringed fingers gripping Caitlin by the arm.

Only the three of them stood outside the compound. The soldiers were still missing, likely hunting Johnny. The men in the room beyond were still cowering, out of sight.

Cora tasted blood on her lip from where she'd bit it. Her head was also throbbing.

The Merchant sneered at her, wiggling his fingers. He now wore a ridiculous crimson suit which was stained with ash marks.

"Up!" he snapped.

She remained motionless, looking for her gun. Then she realized he had it strapped over his ample shoulder.

"Up, now!" he snapped. He tugged painfully on Caitlin's hair. The girl yelped, the gun gouging into her skin.

Cora slowly got to her feet, glaring daggers.

"Your boat," the Merchant snapped. "Take me there. *Now!* Get me off this damn island!"

Cora wanted to protest. Wanted to simply spit on him. But as if sensing her reservation, the Merchant sneered, "Do it, or I blow her head to bits."

Cora shot Caitlin a look. The young woman was still shaking. Cora wasn't sure if her phone call had connected. She spotted her phone on the ground where she'd dropped it. And then, she lied, "Need the phone. The boat has an app-ignition."

"Hurry!" he snapped, shooting panicked looks over his shoulder. "How many?" He asked. "American?"

She followed his gaze, then realized what he meant. "Two SEAL teams," she retorted.

He stared at her, then sneered. "Liar. At least three. Probably more, aren't there? Now go! To your boat. Hurry!"

She gripped her phone. Slipping it into her pocket, she noted where the call had connected and was still ongoing. Her thumb grazed the speaker, turning it on. And then, reluctantly, with rapid glances towards Caitlin, making sure she was okay, Cora broke into a jog, moving back towards the shore.

She took a circuitous route through the trees, all too aware of the gun trained on her spine as she moved. Head bleeding and sleep-deprived, she stumbled on. The Merchant was clearly going to kill them both.

"You know," she murmured slowly as she marched forward, "you should know one thing."

They emerged on the sandy beach. More bodies—ones she hadn't seen before—piled like firewood on the ground, red staining the sand.

She looked for Johnny, tongue wetting her lips.

"Shut up!" he snapped. "Is that it?" he snarled, waving a gun towards the motionless Coast Guard boat. "Where are the others? Where's your team?"

She shook her head, and then, slowly, she turned, staring the Merchant dead in the eyes. "I had a friend once," she whispered.

He leaned forward, "What?"

"A friend," she said quietly. "He was known in the SEALs for his marksmanship. I once saw him—God's honest truth—shoot a single flyaway strand of hair off a balding commander. Cost him five weeks of latrine duty, but he doesn't miss."

The Merchant hesitated now, gripping Caitlin and shooting panicked looks over his shoulder, scanning the tree line.

Cora continued, "Sometimes, you just have to trust the breeze." She was still whispering. She even took a step back.

And he stepped forward, only half a foot. His large, heavy-browed features scrunched over Caitlin's shoulder, the sun glinting off the weapon he pressed to her head. His sneer returned, and as he leaned in to hear her better...

He stepped right into the line of fire.

A *crack*!

A sudden burst of blood.

And the Merchant hit the ground, red speckling the side of Caitlin's face.

She froze, mouth unhinged. A scream caught in her lungs. She stared at the dead man, gaping, panting. Cora approached hurriedly, guiding her away, tugging instantly at the young woman's arm. "Don't look. It's fine. Don't look."

Caitlin continued to hyperventilate, but even still, she murmured, "The others...we have to help the others."

"You hear that, Brady?" Cora snapped, shouting at her phone in her pocket. "Better hurry up. Quickly!"

And then, she looked off to the boat where she had spotted Johnny. He was breathing heavily, panting. His shoulder soaked in blood, but already bandaged with the field kit from the boat. His gun was pressed to his shoulder where he'd been reclining, aiming over the glass.

His dark hair nearly matched the hue of the ash streaking his features.

He gave a fluttering little wave. "It wasn't latrine duty. Was kitchen work," he said, his voice shaking.

Cora snorted and then hastened into the boat, pulling Caitlin along.

"You gonna fall apart, or are you good?"

Johnny flashed a thumbs up. "I'm fine. Just a scrape." He coughed and spat blood over the edge of the boat. "Shit...not sure where that's from. Think that's trouble?"

Cora scowled at Johnny, and he smirked back, his teeth speckled red and black in his grimy countenance. Still, ever the charmer, he took a moment to glance at Caitlin and nod once. "We got you from here. You're going home." He nodded once, his eyes flashing.

Caitlin murmured, "Do you know my mother, too?"

Caitlin and Johnny shared a quick look. *Do you.* Not *did you.*

Cora sighed, gunned the engine, hopped out of the boat, and began to push it back out to sea. Even bullet-riddled, perforated as it was, they'd have to make it the half-hour back to the second island.

"Gonna have to bail, guys," Cora called, gesturing towards a helmet in the back of the boat. "Try to patch up some of those, Johnny!"

"Right, shit—it's already soaking my shoe, Cora."

"Well, bail fast."

"My arm's shot."

"You've got two."

Johnny grumbled. Neither of them addressed Caitlin's comment.

Sometimes when it rained, it poured. And punches came in bunches.

For now, Cora didn't see it as her job to tell Caitlin about her mother. Jamie would have to do that.

Cora had done her part.

Water splashing as Johnny bailed with the helmet and tried to plug

143

the holes with quick-fix sealant, she pulled out of the dock, turned, and pushed the throttle, heading away from the compound. As they fled, she heard a sudden voice, barking authoritatively, on the radio.

"That sound like Columbian military to you?" Cora said, nervously.

"Better go fast," Johnny muttered, grunting as he continued to bail. Caitlin had joined, bailing with her hands.

Cora huffed. At least, by the sound of things—and the glimpse of that large ship coming on the horizon—help was on the way. Good news for the women still on the island.

Bad news if they caught Cora.

But they were a small vessel, nearly sinking. An island was burning.

Comparatively, chances of pursuit were limited.

And so, Cora kept her attention on the horizon, clicking the radio off again. She didn't respond, nor did she look back.

EPILOGUE

Back in the States, Cora sat in her idling car, frowning in the direction of the small bungalow. Johnny was gone. Alive, though, judging by the poop emojis he kept sending her.

She sighed, partially wishing she'd kept that particular line of communication severed.

She was back in Westville. She'd seen the signs on the way in for a new election—a police captain. She sighed slowly, wincing and rubbing at her face. Brady had been trying to contact her, but she hadn't responded.

For the moment, he hadn't ratted her out.

At least, she didn't think so. Nothing had triggered the doorcam back at her apartment. That would have been the first place they raided if they thought she was up to no good.

She sighed, peering through the window of the small bungalow again.

Caitlin had been treated at the hospital. Cora had personally seen her there, but for the last few days, Cora had been hiding, laying low.

And now...

She didn't get out of the car.

She didn't know *why* she remained seated.

But she didn't want to rise. Instead, she just watched through the window, studying the figures within.

Two of them.

One of them was crying, tissues mounding on the table. The other was massaging the weeping girl's shoulders.

Cora felt a lump in her throat.

She wondered how many times Caitlin had cried since coming home...

A home without her mother.

Her aunt leaned across the table, hugging Caitlin, their silhouettes visible through the glass. A third person, Jamie's mother, was busy cooking something on the stove. Cora could just about discern the scent of cinnamon.

145

But this didn't stop the tears.

Caitlin's shoulders were shaking.

Cora had wanted to visit, to stop by and bid farewell. But now...it didn't feel right.

She sat, alone, in the car, watching through the glass. A wall and a window...not much between them.

But enough.

Cora watched a scene she'd seen so often. Different actors and different scripts, but the same declaration—life wasn't easy.

But at least Caitlin wasn't weeping alone. Cora stared through the glass. Partly, she wished she had some money to leave behind. Wished she could help some other way.

But not even Cora could bring the dead back.

She sighed and closed her eyes, leaning her head against the wheel.

She hadn't had a drink or taken a pill all day. And even though her body hurt, she felt...

Strangely content.

The accolades, laurels, and praise were gone. But maybe that was a good thing. Maybe...other avenues were now open to her.

As Caitlin considered this, her mind flashed back.

Another young woman, also with blonde hair and curls.

She felt a lump in her throat that had nothing to do with the scene in front of her. Cora snarled, gunning the engine suddenly, she floored the gas and sped away from the house.

She didn't look back.

Her eyes narrowed, her lips tense as she sped through the streets of Westville, hastening away.

Sometimes, the lost could be found. The forgotten recovered.

And maybe...just maybe...

On *this* side of the law, without a badge for bondage or a bureaucracy for red tape, she had a chance at looking into her own missing person.

Her sister.

Another glimpse of blonde curls, of a smile.

Her best friend.

Missing for almost a decade and a half. Missing, with no answers.

Cora's tires squealed as she turned a corner, blowing through a stop sign.

Maybe, on this side of everything, she would be able to ask the questions that she hadn't been allowed.

Be able to find answers that were otherwise hidden.

She was going back to West Virginia.

Cora nodded firmly to herself. Her family was there, at least, what was left of it.

And it was the place where her sister had vanished. The place where it all had started. She was going to find answers now. One way or another. She *needed* to find answers.

Cora was going home.

But not just that.

She was on the hunt.

NOW AVAILABLE!

UNWANTED
(A Cora Shields Mystery—Book 2)

In this action-packed mystery thriller by #1 bestselling author Blake Pierce, Cora Shields, 30, former Navy Seal turned FBI Special Agent, will stop at nothing to catch a killer—but she is stunned, after bending one rule too many, to find herself fired. When women working for a powerful politician disappear under mysterious circumstances, the cops are too afraid to touch the case, and it's up to vigilante ex-agent Cora Shields to put the pieces together—if she can survive the forces closing in on her.

"A masterpiece of thriller and mystery."
—Books and Movie Reviews, Roberto Mattos (re Once Gone)

UNWANTED (A Cora Shields Suspense Thriller—Book 2) is the second novel in a new series by #1 bestselling mystery and suspense author Blake Pierce

On the outside, Cora Shields is a total badass. A Navy SEAL veteran and a top agent in the FBI's Behavioral Analysis Unit, Cora has a reputation for doing whatever it takes to catch a killer. What no one knows, though, is that she's a wreck on the inside, addicted to painkillers and deeply depressed.

Cora's new case is not what it initially seems, and Cora must enter the dark underworld of crime bosses, gangs, and dirty politicians to uncover the truth at the bottom of it all. But her enemies are watching her closely, and the clock is ticking before another victim is claimed. Can Cora use her skills to crack the case in time?

Or will she be the next woman to disappear?

A page-turning and harrowing crime thriller featuring a brilliant and tortured vigilante, the CORA SHIELDS series is a riveting mystery, packed with non-stop action, suspense, twists and turns, revelations, and driven by a breakneck pace that will keep you flipping pages late into the night.

Book #3 in the series—UNHINGED—is also available.

"An edge of your seat thriller in a new series that keeps you turning pages! ...So many twists, turns and red herrings... I can't wait to see what happens next."
—Reader review (Her Last Wish)

"A strong, complex story about two FBI agents trying to stop a serial killer. If you want an author to capture your attention and have you guessing, yet trying to put the pieces together, Pierce is your author!"
—Reader review (Her Last Wish)

"A typical Blake Pierce twisting, turning, roller coaster ride suspense thriller. Will have you turning the pages to the last sentence of the last chapter!!!"
—Reader review (City of Prey)

"Right from the start we have an unusual protagonist that I haven't seen done in this genre before. The action is nonstop... A very atmospheric novel that will keep you turning pages well into the wee hours."
—Reader review (City of Prey)

"Everything that I look for in a book... a great plot, interesting characters, and grabs your interest right away. The book moves along at a breakneck pace and stays that way until the end. Now on go I to book two!"
—Reader review (Girl, Alone)

"Exciting, heart pounding, edge of your seat book... a must read for mystery and suspense readers!"
—Reader review (Girl, Alone)

Blake Pierce

Blake Pierce is the USA Today bestselling author of the RILEY PAGE mystery series, which includes seventeen books. Blake Pierce is also the author of the MACKENZIE WHITE mystery series, comprising fourteen books; of the AVERY BLACK mystery series, comprising six books; of the KERI LOCKE mystery series, comprising five books; of the MAKING OF RILEY PAIGE mystery series, comprising six books; of the KATE WISE mystery series, comprising seven books; of the CHLOE FINE psychological suspense mystery, comprising six books; of the JESSIE HUNT psychological suspense thriller series, comprising twenty six books; of the AU PAIR psychological suspense thriller series, comprising three books; of the ZOE PRIME mystery series, comprising six books; of the ADELE SHARP mystery series, comprising sixteen books, of the EUROPEAN VOYAGE cozy mystery series, comprising six books; of the new LAURA FROST FBI suspense thriller, comprising eleven books (and counting); of the new ELLA DARK FBI suspense thriller, comprising fourteen books (and counting); of the A YEAR IN EUROPE cozy mystery series, comprising nine books, of the AVA GOLD mystery series, comprising six books (and counting); of the RACHEL GIFT mystery series, comprising ten books (and counting); of the VALERIE LAW mystery series, comprising nine books (and counting); of the PAIGE KING mystery series, comprising eight books (and counting); of the MAY MOORE mystery series, comprising eleven books (and counting); the CORA SHIELDS mystery series, comprising five books (and counting); and of the NICKY LYONS mystery series, comprising five books (and counting).

An avid reader and lifelong fan of the mystery and thriller genres, Blake loves to hear from you, so please email at blake {AT} blakepierceauthor.com to stay in touch.

BOOKS BY BLAKE PIERCE

NICKY LYONS MYSTERY SERIES
ALL MINE (Book #1)
ALL HIS (Book #2)
ALL HE SEES (Book #3)
ALL ALONE (Book #4)
ALL FOR ONE (Book #5)

CORA SHIELDS MYSTERY SERIES
UNDONE (Book #1)
UNWANTED (Book #2)
UNHINGED (Book #3)
UNSAID (Book #4)
UNGLUED (Book #5)

MAY MOORE SUSPENSE THRILLER
NEVER RUN (Book #1)
NEVER TELL (Book #2)
NEVER LIVE (Book #3)
NEVER HIDE (Book #4)
NEVER FORGIVE (Book #5)
NEVER AGAIN (Book #6)
NEVER LOOK BACK (Book #7)
NEVER FORGET (Book #8)
NEVER LET GO (Book #9)
NEVER PRETEND (Book #10)
NEVER HESITATE (Book #11)

PAIGE KING MYSTERY SERIES
THE GIRL HE PINED (Book #1)
THE GIRL HE CHOSE (Book #2)
THE GIRL HE TOOK (Book #3)
THE GIRL HE WISHED (Book #4)
THE GIRL HE CROWNED (Book #5)
THE GIRL HE WATCHED (Book #6)
THE GIRL HE WANTED (Book #7)

THE GIRL HE CLAIMED (Book #8)

VALERIE LAW MYSTERY SERIES
NO MERCY (Book #1)
NO PITY (Book #2)
NO FEAR (Book #3)
NO SLEEP (Book #4)
NO QUARTER (Book #5)
NO CHANCE (Book #6)
NO REFUGE (Book #7)
NO GRACE (Book #8)
NO ESCAPE (Book #9)

RACHEL GIFT MYSTERY SERIES
HER LAST WISH (Book #1)
HER LAST CHANCE (Book #2)
HER LAST HOPE (Book #3)
HER LAST FEAR (Book #4)
HER LAST CHOICE (Book #5)
HER LAST BREATH (Book #6)
HER LAST MISTAKE (Book #7)
HER LAST DESIRE (Book #8)
HER LAST REGRET (Book #9)
HER LAST HOUR (Book #10)

AVA GOLD MYSTERY SERIES
CITY OF PREY (Book #1)
CITY OF FEAR (Book #2)
CITY OF BONES (Book #3)
CITY OF GHOSTS (Book #4)
CITY OF DEATH (Book #5)
CITY OF VICE (Book #6)

A YEAR IN EUROPE
A MURDER IN PARIS (Book #1)
DEATH IN FLORENCE (Book #2)
VENGEANCE IN VIENNA (Book #3)
A FATALITY IN SPAIN (Book #4)

ELLA DARK FBI SUSPENSE THRILLER

GIRL, ALONE (Book #1)
GIRL, TAKEN (Book #2)
GIRL, HUNTED (Book #3)
GIRL, SILENCED (Book #4)
GIRL, VANISHED (Book 5)
GIRL ERASED (Book #6)
GIRL, FORSAKEN (Book #7)
GIRL, TRAPPED (Book #8)
GIRL, EXPENDABLE (Book #9)
GIRL, ESCAPED (Book #10)
GIRL, HIS (Book #11)
GIRL, LURED (Book #12)
GIRL, MISSING (Book #13)
GIRL, UNKNOWN (Book #14)

LAURA FROST FBI SUSPENSE THRILLER
ALREADY GONE (Book #1)
ALREADY SEEN (Book #2)
ALREADY TRAPPED (Book #3)
ALREADY MISSING (Book #4)
ALREADY DEAD (Book #5)
ALREADY TAKEN (Book #6)
ALREADY CHOSEN (Book #7)
ALREADY LOST (Book #8)
ALREADY HIS (Book #9)
ALREADY LURED (Book #10)
ALREADY COLD (Book #11)

EUROPEAN VOYAGE COZY MYSTERY SERIES
MURDER (AND BAKLAVA) (Book #1)
DEATH (AND APPLE STRUDEL) (Book #2)
CRIME (AND LAGER) (Book #3)
MISFORTUNE (AND GOUDA) (Book #4)
CALAMITY (AND A DANISH) (Book #5)
MAYHEM (AND HERRING) (Book #6)

ADELE SHARP MYSTERY SERIES
LEFT TO DIE (Book #1)
LEFT TO RUN (Book #2)
LEFT TO HIDE (Book #3)

LEFT TO KILL (Book #4)
LEFT TO MURDER (Book #5)
LEFT TO ENVY (Book #6)
LEFT TO LAPSE (Book #7)
LEFT TO VANISH (Book #8)
LEFT TO HUNT (Book #9)
LEFT TO FEAR (Book #10)
LEFT TO PREY (Book #11)
LEFT TO LURE (Book #12)
LEFT TO CRAVE (Book #13)
LEFT TO LOATHE (Book #14)
LEFT TO HARM (Book #15)
LEFT TO RUIN (Book #16)

THE AU PAIR SERIES
ALMOST GONE (Book#1)
ALMOST LOST (Book #2)
ALMOST DEAD (Book #3)

ZOE PRIME MYSTERY SERIES
FACE OF DEATH (Book#1)
FACE OF MURDER (Book #2)
FACE OF FEAR (Book #3)
FACE OF MADNESS (Book #4)
FACE OF FURY (Book #5)
FACE OF DARKNESS (Book #6)

A JESSIE HUNT PSYCHOLOGICAL SUSPENSE SERIES
THE PERFECT WIFE (Book #1)
THE PERFECT BLOCK (Book #2)
THE PERFECT HOUSE (Book #3)
THE PERFECT SMILE (Book #4)
THE PERFECT LIE (Book #5)
THE PERFECT LOOK (Book #6)
THE PERFECT AFFAIR (Book #7)
THE PERFECT ALIBI (Book #8)
THE PERFECT NEIGHBOR (Book #9)
THE PERFECT DISGUISE (Book #10)
THE PERFECT SECRET (Book #11)
THE PERFECT FAÇADE (Book #12)

CAUSE TO SAVE (Book #5)
CAUSE TO DREAD (Book #6)

KERI LOCKE MYSTERY SERIES
A TRACE OF DEATH (Book #1)
A TRACE OF MURDER (Book #2)
A TRACE OF VICE (Book #3)
A TRACE OF CRIME (Book #4)
A TRACE OF HOPE (Book #5)

X 22
H 1-23

Made in the USA
Las Vegas, NV
17 December 2022